THE CHRISTMAS FOUNTAIN

A WISHFUL NOVELLA

KAIT NOLAN

For Kady,
Just because Mr. Right turned out to be Mr. Wrong
doesn't mean the Real Deal isn't out there. Keep the
faith, sugar.
Love,
Kait

A LETTER TO READERS

Dear Reader,

This book is set in the Deep South. As such, it contains a great deal of colorful, colloquial, and occasionally grammatically incorrect language. This is a deliberate choice on my part as an author to most accurately represent the region where I have lived my entire life. This book also contains swearing and pre-marital sex between the lead couple, as those things are part of the realistic lives of characters of this generation, and of many of my readers.

If any of these things are not your cup of

tea, please consider that you may not be the right audience for this book. There are scores of other books out there that are written with you in mind. In fact, I've got a list of some of my favorite authors who write on the sweeter side on my website at https://kaitnolan.com/on-the-sweeter-side/

If you choose to stick with me, I hope you enjoy!

Happy reading!

Kait

CHAPTER 1

"MEN ARE WEASELS. AM I right or am I right?"

Mary Alice Reed winced as her cousin, Finn, lifted her Jack and Coke in a toast, and drained half the glass, seeming to take it for granted that everyone agreed. Mary Alice leaned toward their friend Presley and asked, "How much did she have to drink *before* you got her here?"

"It's possible she might have downed a half a fifth of Bailey's. She told me she was having Irish coffee. I didn't realize she'd left the actual coffee out of her mug until she'd drunk most of it."

Mary Alice plucked the glass from Finn's hand.

"Heeeeeey."

"Drink some water so we're not scraping you off the floor in the morning." Mary Alice shoved a full glass in Finn's direction. "And why don't you have some more fries to soak up some of the booze?"

Finn eyed the basket of shoestring fries with a mixture of longing and regret. "They'll go straight to my ass." She sucked the water down by an inch and shrugged. "What the hell? He's not here to care about my ass anymore, is he?"

Mary Alice exchanged a look with Presley. "This is not the night for Margot to be late. Finn's already two-and-a-half sheets to the wind, and we haven't even started The Three Furies."

"Maybe we should reschedule."

"No! We came here tonight to bash my ass-hole ex and tha's what we're gonna do." Finn punctuated each word with a wild gesticulation of the fry.

Mary Alice wiped a splatter of ketchup off the sleeve of her jacket and nudged the water glass. "Drink some more water, sugar."

She scanned the room. The Mudcat Tavern was packed, as it usually was on a Friday night, which meant plenty of witnesses. The Three Furies was Wishful's favorite ritual for the woman scorned. Three shots of booze, three darts, and one unfortunate effigy were supposed to have the cleansing power to put the bastard ex behind you and move on. Mary Alice couldn't understand the appeal of doing such a thing in public. Wishful was a small town, with little better to do than gossip. Why add fuel to the fire?

"I'm so sorry I'm late!" Margot breathed in a rush. "The event ran over and my second in command is out with the flu." The fourth member of their quartet peeled off her winter coat and slid onto a chair, taking a good, hard look at Finn. "Someone got started without me."

"Hail, hail, the gang's all here!" Finn announced cheerfully. She'd grabbed the Jack and Coke, when Mary Alice's back was turned, and drained the glass before they could do anything about it. She slammed it down with a *crack*. "Let's get this party started."

Finn slid off her seat and nearly continued to the floor. Presley caught her, lifting her up with the same wiry strength she used to wrestle recalcitrant dogs at her veterinary practice.

"I'm okay!"

"Are you really? Seriously, Finn, if you can't actually walk to the bar on your own, I'm not letting you do this tonight," Mary Alice warned.

"I'm fiiine," she insisted, pulling away from Presley and turning too quickly, latching onto Mary Alice's sleeve to steady herself. "*You* should be doing this with me." Finn punctuated her statement with a jerk of her arm.

Mary Alice didn't know what the statute of limitations was for completing The Three Furies after a breakup, but three months was probably long past time. Plus, the town loved Judd. He was a damned hero. Coming out in public to complain about how he didn't want her was just going to make her look pathetic. "Thanks, but I'm good."

Finn scowled at her. "No, you're not. If you were good, you'd have moved on by now."

"Just because I didn't run out and try to replace Judd with some other guy doesn't mean I'm not over him."

"How are you not angry?" In her current state, Finn wouldn't understand any woman who didn't want to castrate the offending ex and set him on fire.

"Anger isn't the only way to respond to things."

"You know what your problem is?"

"I have a feeling you're going to tell me."

"You're too damned nice. It's all that time as a teacher. You're all Little Mary Sunshine with your third graders, and it spills over into unhealthy levels of niceness everywhere else."

"It's only unhealthy if it involves denial." And she was done with denial. She'd turned over a new, denial-free leaf. "Enough about me. Tonight is about you exorcising your demons."

"Damn straight." Finn marched toward the bar.

Mary Alice and Margot flanked her, while Presley went on ahead to have a few words with the bartender. A moment later, Adele handed over Bob the Bastard and began pouring the requisite three shots. Presley marched across the bar to the dartboard and fastened Bob to it spread-eagled, as the ritual dictated, for Finn's skewering pleasure. The bar patrons began to cheer and then quieted down for the show.

"Here hangs Seth Turner, Asshole Ex of the First Degree," Presley announced. "Administering his sentence is Finn Watson, the Supremely Wronged Party."

A few women, who were probably veterans of the ritual, booed Seth and called out encouragement to Finn like, "Get the bastard!" and "You go, girl!"

Adele nudged the salt-rimmed shot of tequila toward Finn. "Go on and start forgetting, sugar."

Finn tossed back the shot. Her breath burst out in a wheeze as soon as she managed to swallow. "Holy shit, that's nasty."

Margot handed her the first dart. "List his crimes, sweetheart."

Mary Alice was grateful she hadn't been talked into doing this. Oh, she'd thought about it, during those first few days after the breakup, when she was really angry and hurt. And okay, a few more times as she watched how quickly—and enthusiastically—Judd had moved on. But what would she list as his crimes? Being too dedicated to protecting others? Being meant to be with someone else? Fooling himself? And if he'd been guilty of that one, so had she.

Anyway, it wasn't in her nature to bad-mouth anybody, least of all the man she'd loved.

He wasn't a bad guy. He just...hadn't been her guy in the end.

Finn stepped up to the line, having no such reservations about trashing Seth. Narrowing her eyes at the board, she snarled, "For lying to me, you gutless coward." She let the dart fly. The toss went a little wide, pinning Bob through his left arm and earning a smattering of cheers and applause.

Striding back to the bar, Finn picked up the second shot. Whiskey this time. She threw it back without even blinking.

Mary Alice handed over the second dart. "Cheezits, Mary, and Joseph, woman. I'd be on the floor after all that."

"That's 'cause you're a lightweight."

Because Finn was weaving a little as she went back to the line, Mary Alice stepped back. Current circumstances aside, Finn wasn't a heavyweight in the drinking department herself. She was going to regret this. Mary Alice just knew it.

"For being a selfish asshat." The shot nailed

Bob through one eye, to the collective cheers of the Mudcat's other patrons.

Mary Alice felt a twinge of sympathy for Seth. She didn't know the full story of what had happened between him and her cousin—Finn wasn't ready to talk about the specifics yet—but she'd known and liked him all her life. This whole public spectacle just seemed mean.

Back at the bar, Presley handed Finn the final shot of Jaeger.

"Bottoms up." Finn tossed it back and took the third dart, returning to the line and squinting at Bob. "For being able to walk away." The words were quiet, but the throw was true. She swayed for a long moment, staring at the dart that was still quivering in Bob's heartless chest as the crowd roared its approval.

Mary Alice's heart twisted as she saw the narrow tracks of tears on her cousin's face. All the fight seemed to have left Finn. She stood at the line, shoulders slumped, face pale and drawn. Yeah, Mary Alice remembered that part. She wasn't too far past it herself. She didn't think this was going to be the cleansing ritual Finn had hoped for. Grief took time, and dulling it didn't speed up the process.

Time to get out of here.

Mary Alice reached out, intending to put an arm around her shoulders.

"Oh God." Clapping a hand over her mouth, Finn made a staggering run for the bathroom. People scattered, leaving a clear path for Mary Alice to chase after. She banged her own elbow on the doorframe as she barreled through just in time to see Finn tripping over her own feet and into a stall. Her head cracked sharply against the toilet, as she hit the floor.

"GOD, IT'S QUI—"

A hand slapped over Chad Phillips' mouth. "Don't you dare say the Q word. That's the kiss of death, and you know it."

Chad just quirked a brow at Corinne, the nurse who was filling in for his usual partner in crime in the emergency room of Wilton Memorial Hospital. "Are you seriously not bored out of your mind?" So far, the most serious thing they'd dealt with was a septuagenarian with a shellfish allergy, who'd been in three times in as many months because he didn't understand that removing the crawfish from their shells didn't make them safe to eat. Mr. Spurling's swelling was under control, but Chad wanted to keep him through his antihistamine nap to talk to him *again* about what was and was not appropriate for him to eat.

"I'm caught up on charting for the first time in two weeks," Corinne continued. "I'm not gonna look that gift horse in the mouth. Besides, as long as things stay as they are, I can get out of here at a reasonable hour and maybe actually *talk* to my fiancé before he goes to bed."

Chad felt a spurt of envy that she had someone to go home to. Two someones, as she and her young son had recently moved in with her fiancé. "Is Tucker keeping Kurt tonight?"

"They're taking advantage of my absence for a *Star Wars* marathon."

"Original trilogy?"

"Of course. We're raising him right."

"How are wedding plans going?"

Corinne gave him the side eye. "You *must* be bored if you're asking about wedding plans."

Chad used a couple of pencils as drumsticks to beat a tattoo against the counter. "It's either that, or I'm running down to my office to grab my Nerf basketball set to keep myself awake for the back end of this double shift."

She laughed. "Poor Dr. Phillips. Nights like this make you miss working in metro Atlanta, don't they?"

"True story." He was twitchy with the need to *do something*. He wasn't asking for a big something. No shootings or stabbings. Maybe just some stitches or a broken bone.

"Why *did* you pick such a small hospital? Everybody's heard of your hot-shot reputation. You could've gone almost anywhere."

"I wanted a placement that would give me

time for a life outside the hospital. Atlanta was a constant challenge, and I loved that, but it wasn't worth the trade-off of hours."

"Good for you. Work-life balance is important."

"I wouldn't mind a bit more work to balance out the lack of life side right now."

"The search for Miss Right isn't going well?"

"Eh." Chad shrugged. "I've seen more casseroles and pie than I can shake a stick at. Does that count?"

"I suppose that depends on whether the way to your heart is through your stomach."

Before he could reply, the automatic doors slid open and a gaggle of girls came inside. *Not girls,* he realized. *Women.* He recognized a couple of them in that way lots of faces in this small town were familiar, but he didn't actually know any of them, except for Margot Thayer. He'd met the events coordinator of The Babylon Hotel and Spa several months back during his blessedly brief stint on Dancing With Wishful, a fundraiser for the local women's shelter. She brought up the rear of the party, as two other women supported a petite brunette between them, who didn't seem to be ambulatory on her own.

He could see the knot on her head before he even crossed the room. "What have we got?"

The usually unflappable Margot stumbled over words in her panic. "We shouldn't have let her do it. She'd already been drinking."

The blonde interrupted. "She's completely hammered and fell. Cracked her head on a toilet in the women's room at The Mudcat. We were worried about a concussion." Something in her no-nonsense demeanor seemed vaguely familiar, but he filed that away for later.

The brunette groaned.

"What is it you shouldn't have let her do?" Chad lifted the woman's head with both hands, checking her pulse, even as he looked into un-focused brown eyes. Pupils appeared to be the same size. Her skin was pale and waxy, and she felt clammy to the touch.

"The Three Furies."

"The what now?"

"Series of three shots," the other woman supplied. "Tequila, whiskey, Jaegermeister."

Apparently, there was some kind of a story there, but Chad was more concerned with getting this woman some fluids and doing a more thorough exam. "Let's get her to the back."

Corinne brought a wheelchair.

"Did she lose consciousness at any point?" Chad asked.

The blonde answered again. "No. She was swearing a blue streak almost from the moment she landed."

Chad hunkered down in front of his patient. "What's your name?"

Speaking seemed to take a great deal of effort. "Finn Wasson."

"Watson," the blonde corrected.

Okay, slurred speech.

"Okay then. Finn, I'm Dr. Phillips. We're gonna get you taken care of."

Miserable brown eyes met his, and Finn

promptly vomited on his shoes. Well, he'd wanted something to deal with.

"Has she been vomiting before now?"

Margot knit her hands. "After the Jaeger and once in the car on the way over."

"Can any of you give her medical history?"

"I'm her cousin," the blonde said. "I've probably got the best shot."

"Come with us, then."

The cousin fell into step beside him as he wheeled Finn through the double doors and into the treatment area. As soon as he got the patient settled, he checked the reactivity of her pupils.

"Finn, can you look at me, please? How many fingers am I holding up?" He waved three slowly in front of her face.

She watched for a second, then turned vaguely green and slammed her eyes shut. "Three."

Chad adjusted the bed so she was sitting up and gave her a basin, in case she needed to vomit again. "Corinne, let's get her a liter bolus of normal saline."

The blonde looked up from the clipboard of paperwork she was filling out and bit her lip. "Is she gonna be okay?"

"She'll be fine. A lot of her symptoms could be either concussion or early stages of alcohol poisoning. Getting her rehydrated will help us sort out which. Right now, I'm leaning toward the alcohol poisoning. How much did she drink?"

"The three shots, at least one Jack and Coke, and we think about half a fifth of Bailey's before Presley picked her up. Not sure about anything else."

"Definitely leaning toward the alcohol poisoning."

"I'm just trying to go out with my girls and get over it." Finn's eyes slitted toward her cousin. "She totally should have done this with me. That guy did her wrong. Men are bastards. All men are bastards."

Ooookay. "I gather The Three Furies has something to do with women scorned?"

The blonde nodded, her pale hair shining in the fluorescent lights. Why did she look so familiar?

"It's supposed to be a cathartic experience," she explained.

"Didn't work," Finn announced. "I just wanted to move on, and he's *still* messing with me. And I'm in the damned hospital!"

Corinne came back with the saline and started the IV.

"At least he didn't up and marry someone else six weeks after we broke up like your asshole ex," Finn reflected. "But hell, I don't know. Maybe he did. Maybe he's married now. D'you think he's married now?"

"I doubt he's married, Finn," her cousin said.

"Noooo, you're right. Because that would involve *commitment!* And we know *that's* an issue. What *is* it with men and commitment, Doc? Tell us. As a man."

"Uhhh." Chad clearly had the wrong genitalia to be on the winning side of this conversation. He looked to Corinne for some help, but other than the faintest of twitching at the corners of her mouth, she said nothing.

"Finn." The blonde's tone was somewhere between placating and a warning.

"Not all men. Not all men, I know. Because look at Judd. That's her ex," Finn added, with a pointed look at Chad. "He doesn't have any problem with commitment at all. Two years as a committed boyfriend to Mary Alice here. All the while he's, what, twenty years committed best friend—" She made air quotes. "—to Miss Autumn Buchanan. But nothing going on there. Noooo. Nothing but getting freaking married six weeks after breaking up with you. The bastard."

Six weeks? Talk about ouch.

Color stained Mary Alice's fair cheeks. "Okay, Finn. Let the doctor do his job now."

"You know what I don't understand?" she continued. "Why you're not mad. That's not normal. You're s'posed to be mad. I mean, they're, like, everywhere around town, looking disgustingly happy. A constant reminder."

A flicker of something moved over Mary Alice's face. "I'm more sad than angry. Seeing them together *is* kind of a slap in the face. Like, that should have been me. But it was so obvious, once they finally admitted how they felt about each other, that it could never have been me. He was never mine the way he should have been. And yeah, that sucks, but I don't see the sense in wasting time and energy being angry over the truth. It's not going to turn him into the guy I deserved."

Chad stared at her, feeling such an unexpected sense of kinship, he hardly knew what to do with it.

Finn scoffed. "You're obnoxiously well-adjusted."

Because Mary Alice looked excruciatingly uncomfortable, Chad stepped into the conversational breech. "Well, Ms. Watson, I'm not going to go 'Not all men' on you, but—"

"There's always a but."

"*But*, I had a breakup like that myself back in college. Same kind of deal. And yeah, it sucked to realize she couldn't feel the same about me as I felt about her, but she'd tried for three years. In the end, I realized it would never have worked and was grateful she cut me loose. Although it would've been nice if she'd done it more than a couple months before the wedding."

The patient shoved herself up straight, eyes peeling wide in that way women had with an object of pity. "Oh! Oh, that's terrible. Isn't that terrible, Mary Alice? And you're so pretty."

Chad choked a little. But the spotlight was off Mary Alice, so mission accomplished. She covered her mouth, no doubt to hide the smile he could still see in her pretty blue eyes. It was the sparkle that did it. He snapped his fingers and pointed at her. "Field trip."

Mary Alice dropped her hand. "Sorry?"

"That's where I've seen you before. You were here with your class on a field trip a month or so ago. Elementary school, right?"

"Third grade."

"You're a brave woman."

"Afraid of kids?"

"Only when they run in packs. I can't fathom managing that many of them at one time. Yours were really well behaved."

"Bribery with a pizza party will take you far," she intoned.

He grinned. "It's a classic for a reason."

A throat cleared at the door to the room. "Dr. Phillips, you have a probable broken leg in room two."

"Thanks, Corinne." He rose. "Duty calls. I should be back through to check on you before you leave, but I think it's safe to say it's the alcohol at this point. Once she's done with those fluids, you're free to go, but someone needs to stay with Finn tonight and watch for additional signs of concussion."

"I'm taking her home with me."

"We'll get you a list of what to watch for. Anything else comes up, bring her back."

Mary Alice saluted. "Yes, sir. Thanks, Dr. Phillips."

"You've heard about my ex. I think you could call me Chad."

Her lips curved in a smile. "Thanks, Chad."

By the time he'd dealt with the leg—a spiral fracture that was gonna require a rod and pins, once the guy saw an orthopedist—the room where he'd left Mary Alice and Finn was empty.

"They left about half an hour ago," Corinne told him.

Chad quashed his disappointment. There was no reason for them to hang out in the hospital just because he'd enjoyed talking to Mary Alice. Her cousin was better off resting in a bed at home. "Did Finn look okay when she left?"

"Certainly, better than when she came in. Moving under her own steam to the car."

"Good." He moved to update some notes on the spiral fracture patient.

"Mary Alice left her scarf," Corinne said, with a significant look.

"Keep it at the desk here, in case she comes

back to get it." No doubt it was the last thing she was concerned about after tonight.

"And if she doesn't realize it's missing?"

He held in the grin she was trying to provoke. "I expect somebody can see that it finds its way back to her."

CHAPTER 2

MARY ALICE STILL HADN'T retrieved her scarf by Saturday evening. She might be coping with Finn's hangover or she might simply have been staying inside to avoid the filthy weather. Or maybe she hadn't realized she'd left it behind. Either way, Chad figured he'd make a personal delivery to return the thing. A bold move. Maybe too bold. But he was a man who went after what he wanted, and he told himself it was the neighborly thing to do. People in Wishful were all about being neighborly. Sure, she didn't live by him, but in a town of a little over five thousand people, nobody lived far.

He stood on the front porch of her little bungalow and rang the doorbell, the wind and icy rain lashing at his back. Now that he was here, he wondered what he was going to say. He hadn't much thought past wanting to talk to her again, to see if the sense of connection he'd felt last night was an actual thing or a product of finding someone else who'd been through a situation similar to his. He admired the hell out of Mary Alice's attitude about the whole thing, and he hadn't been able to stop thinking about her. So here he was.

The door swung open to reveal Mary Alice, barefoot, in yoga pants and an oversized Ole Miss sweatshirt. Her fair hair was piled in some kind of messy knot that he found unreasonably sexy. Probably because it looked like she'd rolled out of bed. He didn't want to think about how long it had been since he'd rolled into or out of bed with a woman.

"Dr. Phillips."

When in doubt, smile. "Chad," he corrected. "Unless I'm actually at the hospital, Dr. Phillips makes me think of my dad."

She offered a confused smile of her own. "Do you normally make house calls?"

He laughed a little. "No. You weren't my patient, and that would be weird. I just wanted to bring this by." Reaching into his coat, he pulled out the scarf. "You left it at the hospital last night."

"Oh! I wondered where I'd left it. Thank you." She accepted the scarf, then frowned. "How did you know where I live?"

"Margot told me." And if she'd thought it odd that he'd called her asking, she'd kept it to herself.

The wind kicked up, gusting past him to make her shiver and clutch the scarf to her chest. "You want to come in for a cup of coffee or something? It's freezing out."

"That'd be great, if it's not too much trouble."

She stepped back, opening the door wider

so he could step past her. "It seems the least I can do as thanks for personally delivering my scarf."

He tugged off his beanie and looked around. The entryway opened on the left into a comfortable living room, with the Christmas tree set up in the front window and colorful pillows and throws tossed over the chairs and sofa. To the right was the dining room, currently set with placemats, napkins, and a vibrant red poinsettia. Beyond that, he could just see the kitchen. The whole place just felt cozy, like there ought to be fresh cookies baking, while Bing Crosby crooned from the stereo.

"Nice place."

"Thanks. It's tiny, but it's mine."

He followed her to the kitchen, giving in to the vibe of the place and making himself at home at her table, despite the stacks of office supplies and paperwork scattered across its surface. He hung his wet coat on the back of a chair. "Whatcha working on?"

She glanced over, then popped a K-cup into

the machine on the counter and pressed brew. "Oh, I'm coordinating the details for the Fountain of Hope program."

"And what is that, exactly?"

"It's a Christmas charity for needy children in the community." She kicked back, resting her elbows against the counter, completely at ease in her space. Chad liked that she hadn't flipped out at his unexpected visit and worried about whether the house was picked up or whether she was wearing makeup. Some women he knew insisted on being dressed to the nines and fully made up before stepping outside to get the paper in the morning. Mary Alice didn't need makeup or fancy clothes to be appealing. Her fresh-faced enthusiasm as she spoke was like a breath of fresh air. And the way the position made the sweatshirt stretch across her breasts was tempting all by itself. There was a very nice body under all that baggy clothing.

"Part toy drive, part backpack program, part necessities. There are usually several businesses around town that host donation stations. They put up Christmas trees with printed coins all over them. Each coin represents a particular child. It has the age and gender of the child, along with a list of needs and a few wants. So people can come adopt a child, shop for them, then return the donations to one of those same businesses. Then we wrap and deliver them a few days before Christmas."

"You sound like you know a lot about it."

She set the coffee in front of him with an amused quirk to her lips. "I should. It's my third year chairing it. Cream? Sugar?"

Chad shook his head. "Wow. Sounds like a lot of work."

She grabbed a K-cup from the rack for herself and popped it into the machine. "It is, but it's a cause near and dear to my heart. Several of my students and their families have benefitted over the years. Plus, who doesn't love shopping for kids for Christmas?"

"Fair point." He sipped at his coffee. "Does everything come back to the fountain in this town?"

The fountain at the center of the town green dated back to just after the Civil War. Fed from nearby Hope Springs, it featured heavily in local lore and even heavier in the marketing campaigns currently drawing tourists to town. It had certainly been brought up when he'd been recruited by the hospital here.

"Pretty much."

"Do you buy into the hype? The whole make a wish, and it'll come true business?"

Mary Alice brought her drink—spiced cider from the smell of it—to the table and sat across from him. "I'm a local."

"That doesn't answer the question."

She wrapped her hands around the mug and sighed, the picture of contentment. "It's always been there, in the background. But I guess I've always been too afraid to test the theory."

"Afraid that you'll get what you wish for? Or afraid that you won't?"

A rueful smile curved her mouth. He really liked the shape of that mouth.

"Maybe some of both. There's this whole

implication that the wish has to be made with a pure heart."

"From where I'm sitting, you look like the poster girl for pure of heart."

Color bloomed in her cheeks, and she bent to her drink. "Well, the things I thought about wishing for were a little too self-serving to risk."

Had she thought about making a wish about her relationship with Judd? If he'd had the option back with his ex, would he have risked it to try and save their relationship? No. If she hadn't loved him the way she should on her own, wishing wasn't going to change that. He wondered if Mary Alice had come to the same conclusion.

"So instead you spend your time making other people's wishes come true with your charity."

Mary Alice twitched her shoulders. "Something like that."

Beautiful, charitable, and modest. Exactly the kind of woman he'd like to spend some more time with outside of work. "Are you looking for more volunteers?"

She paused, the mug halfway to her lips. "Are you serious?"

"I came to a small hospital because I wanted to be involved in the community, so that my patients were more than just folders and vital signs." Even as he said it, he felt like an asshat because he hadn't even asked after her cousin.

"We can always use more volunteers. The next meeting is Tuesday at seven, at the community center."

"Speaking of patients, how's Finn? You didn't come back, so I assume she survived the night."

"No other signs of concussion. She's still hung over today, though probably a lot less than she would be without your help."

"I feel like death warmed over." This came from the doorway that led into the hall. Finn stood in pajama pants and a long-sleeved t-shirt. Her dark hair was pulled back into a tail, and her eyes were shadowed. The bruise at her temple was livid. "Little Mary Sunshine here keeps forcing water and painkillers and soup on me."

"Which is probably what's keeping you from feeling like death stone cold," Mary Alice retorted.

"Rehydration and rest is the best thing for you," Chad told her.

Finn turned bloodshot eyes on him. "I'd thank you for making a house call, but clearly you weren't here to see me."

Busted.

"Don't be rude," Mary Alice chastised. "Chad saved your ass last night."

"Didn't know that was gonna turn into an opportunity for him to chase yours."

"Finn!"

That was definitely his cue. Chad shoved back from the table. "I should probably go. Finn needs more rest, and you've got work to do."

The women engaged in some kind of silent communication before Mary Alice walked him to the door. "I'm really sorry about that. It's not personal, she just…"

"Hates all men right now." He smiled a little. "Got that last night. It's fine. And she wasn't entirely wrong. I did come to see you."

Despite her obvious distress over Finn's behavior, she worked up a smile. "Thanks for bringing back my scarf."

"Thanks for forgetting it. I'll see you Tuesday." With one last, long look at that smile, Chad stepped into the rain.

It was a beautiful day.

As a rule, Mary Alice didn't have a temper. It wasn't how she was wired. A good thing, since she spent her days running herd on twenty-five eight-year-olds who could be more than a little trying, at times. But as soon as Chad was out the door, she whirled, marching back into the kitchen, hands fisted.

"That was totally uncalled for."

Finn didn't even look up from the fridge. At least she was voluntarily seeking out food this time. "Just calling it like I see it. So glad you could turn my accident into a chance to scam on my doctor."

"There was no scamming. What does that even mean? I forgot my scarf. He brought it back."

"Convenient," Finn pronounced, sinking down at the table with a slice of cold pizza. "You just happened to leave your scarf. He just *happened* to show up to bring it back."

Mortification chased away the lingering sense of flattery and faint excitement she'd felt when she'd realized Chad had actually wanted to see her. Had he thought she did it on purpose?

"I realize you were completely hammered on Friday, and semi-impaired by a head injury, so maybe you've forgotten, but I was kind of consumed with taking care of you. The last thing I was thinking about was my stupid scarf."

"Y'all were flirting."

"We were *talking*. And anyway, just last night you were just accusing me of not moving on. Carrying on adult conversations with other men is part of that process. Now your nose is out of joint because you think I want to move on with Chad?"

Finn scowled and stared down at her pizza.

"Or maybe you don't want me to move on. Is that it?" Mary Alice asked. "Misery loves company, so you'd rather I be in the same state you are?"

"You were never in this state."

"Because I wasn't visibly angry and bashing Judd and Autumn at every turn? Do you think that means I didn't hurt?"

She threw down the pizza. "How would I know? You never talked about it. You just calmly announced you'd broken up with him, had a little cry, and that was that."

Mary Alice stared at her in exasperation. "Is that really what you think it was like for me? Is that why you're angry with me? Because you think it was easier for me to survive and move on, when you feel like you've been gutted?"

The flicker of shame that crossed Finn's face was answer enough.

Mary Alice didn't want to get into this, but she sat down at the table anyway. "I gave Judd everything for two years. My love, my unwavering support. I didn't complain about the long hours he worked, and I believed him when he said he and Autumn were just friends. To a point, it was true. He never cheated on me. I know that beyond a shadow of a doubt because that's not the kind of man he is. But I was the only one who believed that. So many people warned me off him when we first started dating, and I didn't listen. Because I loved him, and I believed he loved me, or why else would he be with me?"

She wrapped her hands around her empty mug, wishing it was still warm. "When he took me out to The Spring House that last night, he apologized for working so much and talked about making our relationship a priority. He was nervous, and I was so excited because I thought, 'Finally.' And then he pulled out that God-awful bracelet instead of the ring box I was expecting." She could still feel that crushing disappointment. "That, on its own, was bad enough. But the look on his face, when he realized I'd been expecting him to propose made it oh so clear that the idea had never even crossed his mind. And, icing to the cake, he got that call from Autumn and actually *left* me there, at the restaurant, alone. Do you have any idea how humiliated I was?"

Finn had lost the belligerent set to her jaw. She just shook her head. "You never said—"

"No, I didn't. Because it was absolutely mortifying. Nobody predicted that Seth would do what he did to you. *Everybody* predicted Judd would end up with Autumn. I was just too willfully blind to see it. So, no, I didn't do The Three Furies, and I haven't gone around shouting my pain to the skies because I don't want to hear 'I told you so' from anybody. I feel foolish enough without that."

"Mary Alice." Remorse colored Finn's tone.

"And thanks for spilling out all the details to Chad at the ER the other night. Because he might have been the only guy in town who didn't already know that my ex went and *married* his best friend right after I broke up with him."

Finn winced. "I know it's not really meaningful to say I'm sorry for what I said when I was drunk, but I am."

All out of mad and feeling vaguely sick with it, Mary Alice blew out a breath. "It doesn't matter."

"For what it's worth, he didn't look like he was here because he felt sorry for you."

No, he hadn't. "I don't know why he was really here."

"I may be hung over and almost concussed, but even I could see that the pretty, pretty doctor likes you."

Pretty, pretty indeed.

"Maybe. Or maybe he was just being polite." Or maybe he'd be so turned off by Finn's outburst that he'd run the other way. Mary Alice couldn't even blame him.

"Are you really ready to date somebody else?"

Mary Alice shrugged. "I don't know. Nobody's asked. But I'm not still carrying a torch for Judd. He and Autumn were never going to be happy with anybody but each other, and I've accepted that."

"I'd like to get to that point. The acceptance. But right now, I just can't see my way to it."

She laid a hand over Finn's. "By the Girl Code, you still have at *least* another six weeks to bash Seth before you're required to start working through it like a mature adult. So how about I make some brownies and we put on *Kill Bill* and you can talk about how much Seth sucks and what you'd like to do to torture him."

Finn sniffed and turned her hand over to clasp Mary Alice's. "You're a good cousin and friend. Thanks for taking care of me."

"Any time."

CHAPTER 3

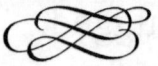

B Y THE TIME CHAD made it to the community center, he was a little bit late. He'd gotten hung up waiting on a patient's test results, not wanting to leave until he could explain what they meant. With no idea how many people to expect, he went straight to the gym, but it was full of rec league basketball and evening walkers on the upstairs track. Back down the hall, he peered through the tiny windows of the doors on each room, finally seeing Mary Alice through the third one he checked. He stepped inside and all heads swiveled in his direction.

At the front of the room, Mary Alice's baby blue eyes widened. "Chad." Was she surprised because she hadn't believed him when he said he wanted to volunteer or because she thought he'd blown it off?

"Sorry I'm late."

After a moment's hesitation, she gestured toward the dozen or so assembled people. "Thanks for coming. Have a seat."

Chad gave her a small nod and quickly found a chair. He could feel the stir around him —the same subtle murmur of surprise and interest he'd learned meant something akin to *Ooo, the new guy's here.* He'd gotten that a lot since he moved to Wishful. How long would it be before he was considered one of them?

"As I was saying, each sponsor business is responsible for setting up their own tree, but I'll need someone to deliver the custom tags, along with the curated list of recipients—which I'm still making, by the way." Mary Alice consulted a clipboard. "I will also need several someones to decorate and drop off the donation collection boxes at each location by Friday."

As she reviewed the list of people and businesses around town who were donating materials and supplies to the cause, Chad looked around the room. He saw Margot and Finn and the other friend who'd been at the ER over the weekend. One of the city councilwomen, Grace Handeford, was also in attendance, along with Cassie Callister, the owner of the local coffee shop, The Daily Grind; and the pastor from the Episcopal Church. More than a half-dozen others he didn't know filled up the rest of the chairs—a mix of men and woman, heavily skewed toward the female.

"We will, of course, have more to do the closer we get to D-Day—"

"D-Day?" Chad asked.

"Delivery day. I have this room booked for the next three weeks, until we make our final drop-offs on Christmas Eve eve, so we can and should utilize it as a work space, not just for storage of supplies and donations. We'll talk more about the later steps at next week's meeting. For now, let's get the immediate assignments done."

Chad shot his hand up. "I volunteer to help you work through the list of recipients and getting the tags made."

She went brows up. "How close do you adhere to the stereotype of doctor?"

"Sorry?"

The corners of her mouth quirked. "How bad is your handwriting?"

He laughed. "Not that bad. And I'm great with computers and spreadsheets. I assume you'll be organizing the list of recipients that way?"

"Something like that. Are you sure? It's a lengthy list, and it's quite the time commitment."

Good. But Chad didn't say that aloud. "Be faster with both of us."

Mary Alice hesitated, scanning the other volunteers, clearly waiting for someone else to speak up. When no one did, she nodded. "Okay, then. We'll coordinate after the meeting." She made a note on her clipboard and went on down the list. She was focused and passionate about her project, and that was just another of those appealing pieces of her he wanted to know more about.

When all the assignments had been handed out, the meeting broke up. Chad hung back, waiting for people to filter out of the room.

Margot approached him. "Well, fancy seeing you here, Dr. Phillips." Her lips curved in an unmistakable smirk. "I gather my directions on Saturday were sufficient to get you where you wanted to go?"

Chad glanced toward Mary Alice, laughing with one of the other volunteers. "Seems like."

Finn strode up and he braced himself for more abrasive commentary on her part. "Doc." She looked uncomfortable. "Sorry for this weekend. I was kind of a jerk."

"Pretty sure nobody should be held accountable for anything they say while drunk or hung over."

Mary Alice joined them. "Are you harassing Dr. Phillips?"

Chad arched a brow. "Are we back to Dr. Phillips?"

"I'm not. They are." Mary Alice shot them a Look and made shooing motions with her hands. "Go."

Their third friend—Presley?—just beamed and herded Margot and Finn out the door.

Mary Alice leaned back against a table, tucking a lock of pale blonde hair behind one ear. "Sorry about them."

His fingers twitched with the desire to reach out and see if her hair was as silky as it looked. "I'm made of tougher stuff. So, the list?"

She blew out a breath. "The list. Look, I appreciate you volunteering, but if this ends up being too much, I get it. No worries."

He shot her a teasing grin. "So sure I'm going to bail."

She didn't smile back. "I understand the demands of an on-call kind of job. I know that plans get made and often broken because the job has to come first, especially when lives are on the line."

How often had Judd Hamilton broken plans and put his job as a cop over her? Judging by the seriousness of her expression, it was standard operating procedure. How long would it take him to prove to her that not every guy was like that?

"Most of my job is not on-call. Not usually, anyway. I have set hours. There are certain occasions, specific conditions that I have more experience dealing with, that I'll get called in for, but it's the exception rather than the rule. I wouldn't commit to this if I couldn't do it. I know you've got a lot of work to do and a short time to do it in, so tell me what you need."

After a long hesitation, wherein she was probably assessing whether she could believe him, she answered, "Well, usually it's just me. I was planning on working on it every day after work between now and Friday to get it done."

"Okay then. I get off at six. How about I pick up a pizza on my way over to your place? Or would you rather meet somewhere else? The Grind? Dinner Belles?"

"All the supplies are at my house, so that's fine. And a pizza would be great."

"What do you like on yours?"

"Italian sausage and peppers."

"How do you feel about adding mushrooms to that list?"

"Amenable."

"Good, because anti-mushroom...that's a deal-breaker."

"Yeah? What are your others?"

"I could never be with a woman who was anti-dog or who doesn't want kids. What about you?"

"Agree on the kid thing. No snoring, must love Christmas, and—" She abruptly busied herself with gathering her things.

"And what?"

Mary Alice shook her head. "It's nothing."

Judging by the sad look in her eyes, it wasn't

nothing, but Chad didn't press. "Let me walk you to your car."

Surprise flickered over her face. "Oh, that's not necessary."

What kind of man did she take him for? "It's after dark. I'm walking you to your car."

The amusement came back. "I dated Wishful's most paranoid and well-trained cop for two years. I have a taser, and he taught me how to use it."

Well, at least Judd had done something to show he cared about her. "It's great that you're well-prepared. But I'm still gonna walk you to your car."

After a moment's hesitation, she angled her head in acquiescence. "Let it be known that chivalry is not dead."

"No ma'am. My mama went to great pains to make certain of it." And he intended to pull out every lesson he'd learned to treat this woman right.

MARY ALICE HAD BEEN out of the general dating pool for a very long time, but she didn't think she was so out of touch that she was mixing up the signals. Despite the less than awesome circumstances under which they'd met, Chad Phillips was interested in her. Why else would he have taken the time to bring back her scarf himself or volunteer for Fountain of Hope?

Well, he had said he was interested in getting involved with the community, but he'd specifically volunteered for the part that would have him spending time with her. That meant he was interested. Didn't it? Or maybe he was just looking to make a friend. He was relatively new in town, after all. Either way, she was vain enough to come home from work and redo her makeup before changing into a sweater and slacks that were a little less elementary school teacher and a little more grown-ass woman who wanted to impress a guy over the age of eight.

Chad arrived promptly at six-thirty, with a carryout box from Speakeasy. He was still in scrubs beneath a zip-up fleece, with faint lines of strain around his eyes, but he had a ready smile for her. "You are the best thing I've seen all day."

A blush heated her cheeks, and she was glad she'd made the effort. "In need of a friendly face?"

"And food. I don't think I had a chance to sit down once since nine o'clock this morning."

He looked worn at the edges, and Mary Alice had the insane urge to hug him. Instead, she stepped back to let him inside. "Let's rectify that."

They settled at the table she'd set with cheerful Fiestaware, loading their plates from the box in the center. He'd inhaled one slice and started on another before his shoulders seemed to relax.

"You want to talk about it?" She expected him to shrug it off, as Judd usually had, drawing a clear line between work life and everything else.

"I'm pretty sure the Universe was making up

for the fact that I dared think it was quiet here. We had a heart attack, two strokes, a ruptured appendix, a concussion, and a construction accident that had me reattaching three fingers, which is where I spent most of the last several hours. I haven't done that kind of detail work in a long time." A faint tone of satisfaction underscored the words.

"You love it."

"Well, I don't wish grievous injury on my patients, but being able to fix it? Yeah, I love that."

"Will the guy regain use of his fingers at all?"

"Not a hundred percent, but it was a clean cut, so he stands a better shot than he might otherwise. It'll be about three months before he starts regaining any sensation. After that it'll depend on physical therapy and luck of the draw. He's a young guy, so that's in his favor, too." He polished off the second slice and reached for a third. "How was your day?"

"Not anywhere near that dramatic. Although Carrie Iverson would probably disagree with me."

"She's one of your students?"

Mary Alice nodded. "Moses Whitwell called her Mouth of the South."

Chad's mouth quirked. "A big talker, is she?"

"She's exceptionally bright, so she often gets through with her work early and tends to socialize. I try to keep some extra things to distract her, but it doesn't always work. Anyway, she was so offended, she made the poor decision to use said big mouth to mock his reading level, which is considerably below hers. The whole class devolved from there." Mary Alice cut herself off. He didn't want to hear about the silly little altercations of her third graders.

"So, what happened?"

She glanced at him in surprise. "You really want to know?"

"Well, you can't just leave me hanging. How does the story end?"

If he was just humoring her to be polite, she couldn't tell. His attention was centered entirely on her, which was such a departure from her last six months with Judd, she realized how much she'd just let slide because it had become their norm. Having an intelligent, attractive man's total focus made her feel a little giddy.

"Well, I had individual sit-downs with each of them, explaining why they were in the wrong. By the time I'd exacted less than sincere apologies from both, we were in the last hour of the day, and I admit my heart was not fully in our discussion of *The Indian in the Cupboard*. Which is disappointing, because it's one of my favorites."

Chad brightened. "I remember that one! The Indian action figure the kid got for his birthday was brought to life by the cupboard. Something about a special key, right?"

"That's the one. We're finishing up this week, in time to watch the movie on Friday. Which is really just a devious plan on my part to occupy them for a couple of hours so I can get a jumpstart on grading."

"Sneaky sneaky. I approve."

"A little deception is necessary when wrangling herds of tiny humans. A huge portion of my job is fooling them into learning stuff, while making them think they're just having fun. It's not reattaching fingers, but it's a different kind of challenge."

"Hey, teaching is one of the most important jobs out there. And often one of the most thankless. You're the front lines with those kids, and you never know which ones you'll have a profound effect on. I think you should be hella proud of what you do."

"Thanks." Faintly embarrassed, she shoved back from the table to take her plate to the sink. "I know you've had a crazy long day. If you're not up to dealing with the list tonight, I completely understand." Mary Alice turned to find him right behind her.

Chad leaned past her to add his own plate to the sink, close enough she could smell the lingering traces of soap and antiseptic, and somewhere beneath that, hints of man. "Why do you keep doing that?"

"Doing what?" He was inside her personal bubble, and she couldn't think straight.

Chad didn't step back. "Creating an out for me. Like you think I've got one foot out the door."

"I'm just trying to be considerate of your other responsibilities."

"I manage my responsibilities just fine, and I wouldn't be here if I didn't want to be." He took a half step closer, so she had to lift her head to keep his gaze.

Awareness hummed along her skin, something she hadn't felt in far too long. It relieved her to know she could feel that for a guy other than Judd, to know she wasn't irrevocably damaged. But she wasn't sure what else she felt about it.

Chad brushed the hair back from her face, his fingers skimming over her cheek. "I'm a patient guy, Mary Alice. If you're not ready, I'm cool with waiting until you are."

She meant to step back, to put some space between them, so she could breathe and think.

Instead, she moved into him, as if his touch were magnetic. Her pulse beat slow and thick as she lifted a hand to his chest. Somewhere in the back of her mind, she could hear her friends cheering her on for getting back out there, but she shut their voices out, focusing instead on his mouth. It was a really nice mouth.

Chad's hand came back to her cheek. "You sure?"

She looked up into his eyes and found them dilated. "Not a bit. But I'm curious." Okay, that might have been a bit more honesty than she'd been going for.

His lips curved. "In the name of science, then." He closed the distance between them, curving his free hand around her waist and lowering his head.

Mary Alice revised her opinion almost instantly. Chad Phillips didn't have a nice mouth. He had an amazing mouth. He didn't rush, didn't push. Instead, he applied all that exceptional focus to the play of his lips over hers. The man had said he had patience. He showed all that and then some as he took his glorious time, as if he had no other purpose in life than learning every millimeter of her mouth. She relaxed into him on a sigh, her body going pliant and her traitorous knees turning to jelly in a level of surrender she hadn't planned, hadn't expected. And that surrender seemed to shift something in him, a spark to bone-dry tinder. He slanted his mouth, tracing her lips with his tongue. She opened for him, relishing it as he took the kiss deeper. The body that had been lax went taut, her hands fisting in his shirt as she caught fire.

What seemed like moments after he'd lit the flame, Chad eased back, leaving her dizzy and wanting. "I'd say that proves our hypothesis."

Her heart beat an unsteady tattoo in her chest, and it took her a moment to find her voice. "Which hypothesis was that?"

"That we have chemistry."

"Oh, that hypothesis." Yeah, he'd proved that pretty conclusively. And she didn't know how she felt about it. Willing tension back in her knees, Mary Alice made herself uncurl the fingers that were white-knuckling his shirt and step back from him. "That's certainly something to think about." She suspected that little experiment was going to be playing on repeat in her dreams for the rest of the week, at least.

His smile was understanding, even as banked heat lingered in his eyes. "Take all the time you need. And consider me available for any further experimentation you deem necessary."

Mary Alice laughed. "I'll keep that in mind. Meanwhile, we should get started on that list."

"As you wish."

CHAPTER 4

$\mathscr{I}$T TOOK LONGER FOR Chad to break free of the ER than he'd planned, so he made it only for the tail end of Mary Alice's presentation to hospital staff on Fountain of Hope. She was explaining how to fill out the paperwork that would allow people to adopt a child for the holiday season. He slipped in at the periphery, where he could watch and listen.

"Each coin has been anonymized, so it's important that the people doing the record-keeping make note of the identification number on each coin before releasing it to adopters."

Chad and Mary Alice had spent long hours after work the last two days getting all the coins filled out for each child and divided up for each participating local business. Long hours they'd spent talking about anything and everything. He knew someone else was doing the drop-off and explanation of process everywhere else, but Mary Alice had made the time to come to the hospital. He hoped she'd made the effort because of him.

She hadn't spooked after their kiss—not exactly. But she'd clearly needed room to process, so he'd focused on the business at hand rather than finding a way to get his mouth back on her. But he'd thought about that kiss and her. It had been a helluva kiss.

"Any more questions?" She looked around, waiting, and Chad started easing through the pack toward her. "Okay, hearing none, I'll simply say thank you for your participation!

You're going to help make a lot of children's lives brighter this holiday season."

The crowd broke apart, heading back to their duties, and Mary Alice finally caught sight of him. Her sunny smile was a serious bright spot to a very busy day.

"Hey! I didn't see you back there."

"Got caught up, but I managed to sneak in for the end. Buy you a cup of coffee?" He was aware of the raised eyebrows from a trio of lingering nurses.

"Isn't hospital coffee supposed to be terrible?"

"Only the stuff in the vending machines. The cafeteria is a different matter. It's not The Grind, but it's pretty good."

"I could do with a pick-me-up," she agreed, falling into step with him.

He led her downstairs. "How did the kids like the movie?"

Mary Alice glanced over, brows lifted. Did she think he'd already forgotten?

"Loved it. It's a pretty decent adaptation of

the book. Best of all, I finished all my grading for the weekend, which is cause to celebrate."

Chad filed that little detail away as they reached the cafeteria. He took her through the line, grabbing his own cup of medium roast and waiting, while she doctored hers with cream and two sugars. He filed that away, too, as they went to check out. "Hey there, Louise. How's your day going?"

"Just fine, Dr. Phillips." The older woman looked Mary Alice over, then gave him a nod of approval enthusiastic enough to make her tower of silver hair shiver.

Chad just grinned. "Louise, this is Mary Alice Reed. She's heading up Fountain of Hope this year."

"Chad's been a big help."

"Nice to meet you, honey. Good to see someone getting this one involved in the community. He needs more life outside the hospital." Louise pursed her coral-painted lips and arched both brows, as if to say she knew exactly how much time he spent up here. Which probably wasn't far from the truth.

He swiped his ID badge to pay. "I'm working on it."

They sat at one of the tables by the long bank of windows. Mary Alice took the top off her coffee and blew. Because he knew exactly how fast he could get pulled away, he did the same.

"So, it seemed like your presentation went pretty well today."

"There are several folks here who've participated in years past, so that helps. They know the ropes already."

"The hospital seems kind of an odd place to set up. I'd think most people coming through here are preoccupied with whatever brought them in."

She angled her head in concession. "You're not wrong. Most of the children who get adopted from here are adopted by the staff. It makes sense because they often can't get out to one of the other locations due to work, which you know something about."

"Fair point. What about you? Do you ever end up adopting a kid from the program?"

"Usually several. Often former or current students. It's technically cheating that I know who I'm shopping for, but I love it because I know them, and I can personalize a bit more."

She was a school teacher in one of the poorest states in the country, so she couldn't be making much. But she gave back on so many levels. It impressed him. She impressed him.

"That's both generous and awesome."

Mary Alice shrugged. "It's a lot of fun."

The PA crackled. "Dr. Phillips, you're needed in the ER. Dr. Phillips, you're needed in the ER."

"Damn. Sorry," Chad muttered. He'd hoped for a longer lull before springing back into action.

"Duty calls. Go save a life."

He looked at the barely empty coffee cup and deemed it cool enough to chug. Gulping all of it, he rose with an apologetic smile. "To be continued."

Mary Alice waved.

Reluctant to let her out of his sight, he backed toward the exit. "Spend tomorrow with me," he called.

"We just hung out the last two nights."

That had Louise's interest piquing.

"That was work. I wanna take you out."

"Like a date?"

"Not like a date. On a date." He'd meant to give her more time to acclimate, but he just didn't want to wait.

"Come on, child. This one's a catch," Louise added.

"You said you finished your grading. C'mon. Say yes, Mary Alice."

After a long second, she smiled. "Okay then. Tomorrow."

When he pumped his fist in victory, she laughed, and he carried the sound of it with him as he ran for the ER.

Mary Alice climbed out of Chad's SUV and looked over the rolling hills of Applewhite Christmas Tree farm. As a location for their date, it was entirely unexpected. She loved it out here, miles from town, surrounded by the crisp scent of evergreens. "I have so many fond memories of coming out here with my family as a kid."

Chad came around the front of the vehicle and took her hand. "Why did y'all stop coming?"

"I don't know. Just grew up, I guess. I brought my class out here on a field trip one year."

"I bet they loved that."

"You bet. But what are we doing here? Are we cutting a Christmas tree? Because, in case you missed it, mine is already up." The prelit one had come out of the box the day after Thanksgiving. She appreciated the convenience and longevity of a fake tree and, God knew, not having to untangle lights was a blessing. But standing out here, she remembered all the reasons she loved real ones.

"Now that you mention it, we should do that while we're here. I haven't got one yet. But no, that's not why." He tugged her toward the barn, where Jace Applewhite was watering a team of horses hitched to a hay wagon. He'd been a few years behind her in school, but she remembered him.

"Everything ready?" Chad asked him.

Jace grinned. "Tara and the kids are just getting back." He nodded behind them, toward the fields.

Mary Alice turned and saw a tall, blonde woman, a lanky boy, and a familiar little girl striding out from the rows of trees. The little girl broke into a run. "Miss Reed! Miss Reed!"

"One of yours, I presume?" Chad asked.

"Last year." Mary Alice crouched, arms open to catch the child as she rocketed in for a hug. "Hey Ginny! How are you?"

"I'm awesome! Next week, when school's

out, we're moving out to the tree farm for Christmas, on account of Tara's dating Jace and we're honorary Applewhites."

"Well, that just sounds like a blast."

"Second year out here," Tara said, slipping an arm around Jace's waist.

"That makes it tradition," Ginny declared.

"That it does," Jace agreed, ruffling her hair.

"Maybe we'll get a repeat of last year's white Christmas," her brother Austin added hopefully.

"Your mouth to God's ear," Mary Alice laughed.

It was good to see them happy. When their father had gone to prison for burglary, Tara had left college to become guardian to her two half-siblings. Mary Alice knew better than many the tough road they'd travelled. She'd had several conferences with Tara last year. It seemed that after a rough start, they'd finally found their groove as a family.

As a minivan pulled up, Jace nodded toward it. "Austin, you want to handle this one?"

"On it." The boy headed for the family piling out of the van, a broad smile in place and the spiel clearly ready on his tongue.

Tara pulled something from her coat pocket and handed it over to Chad. "Before I forget."

He held up the little scroll tied in Christmas ribbon. "This wasn't what I left you."

"My version is better," she said. "You don't get an artist involved in your scheming and not expect her to fancy it up a bit."

Mary Alice folded her arms, narrowing her eyes at Chad. "What are you up to?"

"We're going on a scavenger hunt."

"A scavenger hunt?" She grinned at the idea of it. She hadn't been on one since she was a kid at camp. How on earth had he put together something like that since yesterday afternoon?

"You've been working your butt off this week, so I thought you could do with an adventure. I had to recruit a little help. Thanks for that, by the way," he said to Jace and the others.

"Anytime, man. You saved my dad's life."

"Is he taking it easy, as ordered?"

"Mom's got an eagle eye on him. He's grumbling a lot and doesn't think much of the heart healthy diet, but he's doing better."

"Good to hear."

"Y'all should be getting on," Tara said. "You don't want to lose daylight before you're ready."

"The plan calls for being out here after dark?" Mary Alice asked.

"You did promise the day."

"So I did." Now that she knew what he'd been up to, she understood why that day had started later than expected.

He handed over the scroll with a flourish. "Your first clue, milady."

Mary Alice slid off the ribbon and unrolled the parchment to find a few lines of gorgeously rendered calligraphy. She read the clue aloud.

"My branches are lovely, or didn't you hear?

Santa's helper is waiting, and I don't mean his reindeer.

(Though their number will give you the right row.)"

She laughed. "It's a tree farm. Everything is trees planted in rows."

Ginny did a little dance. "It's—"

Tara clapped a hand over her mouth. "Get going before she spoils it. This one's terrible at keeping secrets."

Ginny tugged her hand away. "Am not!"

"How about you go get some carrots out of the crisper for Rupert and Pepper?" Jace suggested.

The girl huffed. "Fine. Have fun, Miss Reed!"

"I will. Thanks for your help!"

"It helps if you sing!" she called, as she jogged toward the house.

"Sing," Mary Alice muttered. She read the clue over. "O' Christmas tree, O' Christmas tree, how lovely are thy branches. Ah. To the tree fields."

Chad grabbed a tree tag, and they headed out.

"It should be the..." She counted off on her fingers. "Dasher, Dancer, Prancer, Vixen, Comet, Cupid, Donner, Blitzen, Rudolph—

ninth row. But ninth counting from which side?"

"Don't look at me. I'm not the one who did the hiding."

"Logically, I guess I'd start counting from the side closest to the house."

"Seems a reasonable guess." Chad took her hand again as they walked over to the ninth row and began to search its length.

A few other families and couples were browsing for their perfect tree. She'd wanted to come back out here with Judd, but cell reception was spotty, and with Autumn's heart condition, he'd never been willing to be out of contact that long.

"What's wrong?" Chad asked.

Mary Alice shook off the shadow on her mood. "I was just thinking of some of the other reasons I haven't been back out here since I moved home. It's not important. They weren't good reasons." She worked up a smile for the thoughtful man who'd brought her. "Have you ever cut your own tree?"

"Can't say I ever had a Paul Bunyan moment, though we do always get a live tree in my family. We've got vaulted ceilings in my parents' house, so Mom always gets the biggest Frasier fir you can imagine off the lot."

"We should find you one. How tall are your ceilings?"

"Nine or ten feet, I think."

They circled each tree, searching for clues, even as they evaluated the height and shape. Halfway down the row, nestled in the branches of a beautiful Frasier fir, they found the next clue dangling from the hand of an adorable elf ornament.

"How cute is this!" Mary Alice carefully unhooked it, turning it over in her hands.

"It's a good tree, too."

"You should tag it."

He fastened his tag as she unrolled the next strip of parchment and read.

"*We are a component of this favored cold-weather brew.*

Come to our center and find something for you.

"Cold-weather brew. Well, they don't have cows here, so it has to be spiced apple cider. Middle of the apple orchard."

Chad made an exaggerated after you gesture. "Lead the way, madam."

Getting into the spirit of things, Mary Alice grabbed his hand this time. She enjoyed the feel of his fingers curving around hers, the easy swing of their arms as they walked. Despite the low-level hum of awareness she felt around him, it was comfortable.

"Tell me about your family," she said. "Big? Small? In-between?"

"In-between, I guess. Mom, Dad, and one younger brother, Hale."

"Did he follow in the family footsteps and become a doctor, too?"

"No. He resented the hell out of all the time Dad spent away from us at work. He's a glass artist." Chad's tone was light, but Mary Alice sensed some resentment on his part, too. "What about you?"

"Same. Mom, Dad, little sister. Bethany's in law school at Ole Miss."

"Do y'all get along?"

"Oh, we fought, as sisters do. But we're better as adults. We agree that we definitely want different things out of life. She longs for the city and the thrill of battle in court. I'm good with a small-town life. I like the continuity of generations and the lifelong friendships."

"I find that very appealing. It's not at all what I grew up with in Atlanta."

She glanced up at him. "Does your family think it odd that you chose a small town?"

"Just Dad. He thinks my skills are wasted here."

Mary Alice squeezed his hand. "I'm sure the guy whose fingers you reattached this week wouldn't agree."

Chad smiled and brought her hand up for a quick kiss. "And neither do I."

Their target was more easily spotted in the apple orchard. A toy locomotive engine dangled from a branch, and nestled in the crook of the tree was a huge, stainless-steel thermos. The next clue was tucked through the windows of the train. As the temperatures were starting to drop along with the sun, Mary Alice twisted open the cap, surprised to find hot chocolate.

"I totally expected hot cider."

"It fit for the clue but not the theme of the rest," Chad explained.

"There's a theme?"

"There is." His mouth lifted, his eyes sparkling.

"An elf, a train, and hot chocolate..." Mary Alice gasped and wondered if she put it together right.

"Do you want to guess?"

"No. I'm waiting until I see what's next." She handed over the thermos and unrolled the parchment.

"In summer, you'll find shade under our span
Tonight's final stop is our grove of_____.
The only other kind of grove they have is pecans." Mary Alice frowned. "That doesn't

rhyme."

"It does if you're from Georgia."

"This is Mississippi, city boy. Here we say pe-KHAN. Which is the correct way."

Laughing, he wrapped an arm around her as they headed toward the pecan grove. "How about we agree to disagree on the proper pronunciation and agree that pecan pie is damned tasty in any incarnation?"

"I can accept that compromise."

They shared a capful of the hot chocolate on the walk, discussing favorite desserts and family recipes. The sun was down by the time they made it to the backside of the grove and the shed at its edge. They circled around to the other side and Mary Alice gasped in delight.

A fire pit was ready and waiting to light. A picnic hamper and blanket lay neatly to one side. But that wasn't the best part. A white sheet was hung from the back wall of the shed, and a projector was attached to a laptop, just waiting to play.

"This is...amazing."

Chad just grinned. "You want to take that guess now?"

"Did you set all of this up for a private viewing of *The Polar Express*?"

He crouched down and lifted the lid on the basket, pulling out the Blu-ray.

Tears stung Mary Alice's eyes. "You did all of this for me?"

"A little bird told me it's your favorite Christmas movie."

"Which little bird?"

"Margot," he admitted sheepishly. "Do I lose points for consulting?"

He'd asked her friend what she'd like and gone to an enormous amount of trouble to create something unique and special sur-rounding that. For her. Judd had never made that kind of effort. Riding on emotion, she pulled Chad to his feet and into a kiss. She poured out everything she wasn't quite ready to say, hoping he understood what it meant to her for someone to make her feel special. His arms came around her, and he pulled her closer, deepening the kiss she'd only meant as thanks. Mary Alice was helpless to do more than answer.

They were both breathing hard when they broke apart.

"So, I'm gonna go out on a limb and say I maybe didn't lose points?"

She laughed. "You gained so many points, it's not even funny." With another quick squeeze, she stepped back. "Seriously, thank you. This is beyond amazing."

He winked. "Wait until you see what other surprises are in the basket."

Mary Alice was pretty sure the biggest surprise was him, and she couldn't wait to find out.

CHAPTER 5

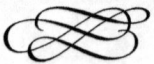

"EXCUSE ME. SIR? SIR!"

Chad paused in the hallway of Wishful Elementary, as a woman hurried after him, a pair of reading glasses bouncing on a chain around her neck.

"Can I help you?" she asked.

"No, I'm good. I'm on my way to Mary Alice Reed's classroom."

"Are you one of the parents helping out this week?"

"No, I'm Chad Phillips—" The words "her boyfriend" were on the tip of his tongue, but that was getting ahead of things after only one formal date. "—a friend. But I am helping out."

Her expression didn't change at his name, so evidently, she wasn't up on all the latest gossip. "You can't just wander around the school without checking in at the office. Miss Reed should have told you."

He offered what he hoped was a disarming smile. "I'm sorry. I wasn't aware. I was surprising her."

The woman's eyes narrowed. "Come with me."

Her tone had Chad resisting the urge to hunch his shoulders. He felt like he'd been called to the principal's office. As he followed her back toward the entrance, he realized school was apparently a lot different than it had been when he was a kid.

He didn't see any familiar faces among the office staff as he was told to sit. The woman who'd chased him down lifted the receiver on a phone and punched in a few buttons. "Miss Reed, can you please come down to the office?"

Well, hell. He hoped he hadn't just gotten her in trouble, too.

A few minutes later, Mary Alice stepped into the room. "I hope this won't take long. The kids are—" She caught sight of him. "Chad? What are you doing here?"

"You said your aide was out sick, so I did a little rearranging of my schedule this afternoon to come help with the ornament making. I was going to surprise you, but apparently that's verboten."

"That's incredibly sweet." She gave him that smile he was starting to crave. "Please let Dr. Phillips sign in, y'all. We need to get back before the kids start hanging from the ceiling. They're wild today."

At the mention of doctor, eyebrows were raised and looks were exchanged. He was pretty sure the secretary whispered, "You go girl," to Mary Alice as he finished signing in.

Once they were headed back to her classroom, he said, "Sorry about this. I didn't know my walking in would set them to DefCon 4."

"We take security seriously, even here in a small town."

"I hope you're not in trouble."

"No, it's fine. Principal Schumaker loves me."

"So I did get called to the principal's office."

She laughed. "New experience for you?"

"I might have had a little experience back in the day." He thought about taking her hand but considered that probably wasn't appropriate in her workplace.

They stopped just outside a classroom, and Mary Alice turned to face him. "What are you really doing here?"

"I missed you. Isn't that enough?"

Her face softened in that way that said her Awww Meter was pinging. But, hell, it was the truth.

"Hang on to that thought." She opened the door, and they stepped into chaos.

Kids were out of their seats everywhere. At least three were running. As Chad came further into the room, a paper airplane zipped inches in front of his face. And the noise. Good lord. Mary Alice waded in, clapping her hands. When that didn't get any response, she stuck two fingers in her mouth and let out a whistle worthy of any major league umpire. Chad decided he was half in love with her. The kids immediately shut up and went back to their seats.

"That's better. Class, I'd like to introduce you to Dr. Phillips. He's here to help us out this afternoon with our ornament project."

He gave an easy wave. "Maybe just Dr. Chad."

A hand shot up in the back of the room.

"Yes, Aidan?"

"What kind of doctor are you?"

"I'm in emergency medicine. So, if you get hurt and have to come to the emergency room at the hospital, it's me you see." He didn't see the sense in explaining that he was actually a trauma surgeon. That wasn't his primary role here.

"Dr. Chad reattached somebody's *fingers* last week," Mary Alice told them.

This elicited a chorus of ooos and aaaahs and promptly led to at least four kids opening their mouths to ask questions, but Mary Alice skillfully intervened before they got completely off track.

Fifteen minutes later, he was sitting at a low table with a trio of the most curious as Mary Alice passed out portions of salt dough.

"This is *not* cookie dough, y'all. It's made with salt instead of sugar, so it's gonna taste terrible. But it'll bake up nice and strong in whatever shapes you like." She went over various suggestions—Christmas trees, candy canes, reindeer, angels, snowmen, and the like. "I'll take them home and bake them tonight, and we'll paint tomorrow."

As they settled in to work, the little boy across the table, who'd introduced himself as Isaiah, fixed big, dark eyes on Chad's face. "I'm gonna be a doctor when I grow up."

"Yeah?"

He nodded, expression serious as a judge.

"Gonna learn all about how to put people back together, so I can fix my Gramma."

Chad felt his heart crack a little bit. He had no idea what was wrong with the boy's grandmother, but suspected whatever it was, she probably wouldn't make it through this child growing up to graduate med school. His own expression sober, Chad said, "That's a good goal. I bet she'd be real proud of that."

The other two interrupted with a rapid-fire series of questions about the biggest thing he'd ever reattached, the grossest thing he'd ever seen, and whether he could bring people back from the dead. They were surprisingly ghoulish for what he'd expected from eight-year-olds. He chatted and molded, helping when asked and otherwise braiding together several long ropes of dough to make a wreath.

Mary Alice peeked over his shoulder. "Nicely done, Dr. Chad. That's gonna look really nice on your tree."

He hoped she'd help him decorate it.

At the end of the day, the kids declared it

best day ever and asked if Chad could come back tomorrow. He'd have been lying if he didn't admit to feeling a glow of pleasure at their enthusiasm.

"Not tomorrow," Mary Alice told them. "Dr. Chad has to go back to work at the hospital. But if you're really good, maybe he can come back sometime when we get back from Christmas break."

When they bolted from the room at the final bell like a pack of over-exuberant puppies, Chad began moving around the room, picking up supplies, as Mary Alice carefully put ornaments on a tray and covered them with plastic wrap.

"You were really good with them today."

He glanced up at her. "You sound surprised."

"A lot of guys don't know what to do with kids."

"Kids are people, too. Just shorter."

She laughed. "True enough."

"I like kids. Want a couple of my own someday. What about you?"

Something that might have been regret passed over her face. "I kinda thought I'd have been started on that already. But, yeah, someday."

Still a tender spot, he thought. "Tell me about Isaiah. His grandmother is ill?"

Mary Alice sobered. "She's the primary caregiver in his family. His dad hasn't been in the picture, and his mom is in and out. His grandmother is the constant. She's got fibromyalgia. It's amazing what she's managed under those conditions."

Chad wondered who her primary physician was and whether he could do anything to help.

"Isaiah is one of our Fountain of Hope kids."

"I want him." He felt a connection with the boy. Maybe, in the grand scheme of things, this wouldn't be a huge thing, but it was what he could do now to maybe make the kid's life a little brighter.

She smiled. "I've already got him." Stepping into him, she slid her arms up to link around his neck. "But I could probably be induced to share."

Chad pulled her close. "Yeah? What are your terms?"

"We should discuss that over dinner."

Touching his brow to hers, he sighed in contentment. "That is the best idea you've had all day."

THE DAILY GRIND was hopping Saturday morning, when Mary Alice stopped by to pick up coffees on her way over to Chad's. They were headed to Lawley, the bigger town about forty-five minutes away, to do their shopping for Fountain of Hope.

Cassie Callister, the owner of the coffee shop, was bustling behind the counter with all the speed of a woman hooked up to an IV drip of espresso. "Hey Mary Alice, what can I get you?"

"I'll have whatever you're having. I could use

a boost this morning." Maybe it would make up for the lack of sleep she'd been getting the last couple of weeks because she and Chad had been staying up late every night working or talking. Crazy how fast that had become part of her routine.

Cassie ran her fingers through her turquoise streaked brown hair and laughed. "It's an I Can't Do This Anymore. Pretty high octane compared to what you usually drink."

"I'm living dangerously this morning. And let me get a large whatever your darkest roast is at the moment. Both to go."

"You got it." She whirled away and began pushing buttons and pulling levers with speed and efficiency. Mary Alice thought it looked a bit like a dance. A couple of minutes later, she set the first cup on the counter. "And is this other one for Dr. McHottie? I heard you've been seeing a lot of him the last couple of weeks."

Dr. McHottie? The nickname would amuse

him. Mary Alice smiled. "Yeah, it's for Chad. He's been a big help with Fountain of Hope."

"I'd heard things were a bit more personal than that. That you two were dating. C'mon, girl, I was in that committee meeting! I saw the way he looked at you. Dish." Cassie, with all her good-humored enthusiasm, was in a constant battle with Mama Pearl, the proprietress of Dinner Belles Diner, for the title of Wishful Gossip Queen.

Mary Alice thought about the special scavenger hunt he'd put together for her and about how he'd rearranged his work schedule to come help in her class. And the kissing. Yeah, she couldn't claim to be doing *that* with any of her other committee members. "I suppose we are."

Cassie slid Chad's coffee next to the first. "Good for you, honey! I'm glad to see you back out there."

"Thanks?" She added a couple of muffins to her order and paid. It felt weird having people who weren't her best friends opining about the state of her love life. But, good or ill, she supposed it was better than having them talk about her in pity. Stepping over to the beverage station, she popped the lid off her coffee and began to doctor it. From somewhere behind her, she heard Chad's name mentioned.

"Well, I just think it's a shame, is all. Everybody knows she's just using him as a rebound after all that mess with Judd."

"Helluva rebound," someone answered.

Mary Alice went stiff. Was this really what people thought? That she was using Chad as her rebound guy? She didn't look to see who the speakers were. She didn't want to know. Instead, she took her tray of coffees and the bag of muffins and escaped.

On the drive to Chad's, she tried to put the whole thing out of her mind, but it continued to circle around her brain.

He'd apparently been watching for her because he came out of the house as soon as she pulled into the driveway. With a cheerful smile, he slid into the passenger seat of her Nissan Rogue. "Good morning, beautiful." Leaning across the console, he caught her mouth for a kiss that had her pulse doing a tap dance.

Warmth pooled low in her belly as she reached up to cup his cheek. Stubble rasped against her fingers and had her thinking about late nights involving something a lot more personal than work or phone calls. Even before she'd broken things off with Judd, it had been months since they'd been intimate. Needs she'd repressed or ignored came roaring back to life, and along with them the echo of the gossips she'd overheard.

Rebound.

Mary Alice broke away and blew out a breath. "Good morning to you, too. I like the scruff." Surely, this attraction she felt was the real thing and not some product of her touch-starved brain.

Chad scrubbed his hand over his jaw. "Got called in for a late surgery last night. Didn't take too long, but I wasn't much in the mood to shave this morning."

"Oh, are you too tired? We can reschedule."

"I've been looking forward to spending today with you all week. I don't want to reschedule."

How could she not be into a guy who said stuff like that? "I got breakfast."

He peered into the bag and pulled out one of the gigantic blueberry streusel muffins. "Mmm, these are my favorite."

"I'd say lucky guess on my part, but they're everyone's favorite." Mary Alice backed out of the drive and headed for the highway.

He made a few volleys at conversation, then lapsed into silence when she failed to pick up any of the topics and run with them. She liked that he'd let her be alone with her thoughts for a bit, that they could sit in comfortable silence —even if her head wasn't in the greatest place.

Somewhere around Chapel Creek, he finally spoke again. "I don't think I've ever seen you with a frown before. At least not while sober. What's wrong?"

She considered blowing it off, but she'd blown off too many things, made too many excuses in her relationship with Judd. She didn't want to make the same mistakes. "Do you think, when you get out of a long relationship, that whatever relationship immediately follows is automatically a rebound?"

He considered the question. "I think that's a gross over-simplification. Some people get out of one relationship and immediately look to fall into another, without taking the time to sort out what went wrong. They're too afraid of being alone. But I think others actually take the time to do the work to learn from the failed relationship, so they're in a better place for entering into a new relationship, when it comes around. Are you worried that's what this is? That I'm your rebound guy?" His tone was neutral, revealing nothing about how he felt about the possibility.

"I hadn't even thought about it. But some people were gossiping about us at The Grind and it just...bothered me." Mary Alice glanced over to find his kind eyes fixed on her. "I find you appealing on pretty much every level.

You're smart, funny, gorgeous, and incredibly considerate. Spending time with you, being the focus of your attention—it's all exciting and new and fun. I'd be lying if I didn't admit it's gratifying to my wounded ego." She swallowed, grateful to be able to fix her attention on the road. "I feel like I've done the work. I know exactly what went wrong in my last relationship. So no, whatever this is happening between us, I don't feel like it's a rebound." She shot another quick glance in his direction. "I hope it's just the start of the next real relationship."

Heat flooded her cheeks. She hadn't meant to say that aloud. Not this soon. But she didn't take it back. It was true. She wanted a real relationship with Chad, and she didn't expect to feel that so quickly after Judd.

"Is that what you want this to be?"

Mary Alice bit the inside of her lip. She'd spent too much time not saying what she wanted with Judd. "Yeah. I mean, that's probably getting ahead of things. It's only been a couple of weeks, but—"

Chad picked up her hand and kissed it. "It's what I want, too."

Relief came first, and on the heels of it, her smile spread wide. "Okay." She laced her fingers with his. "Let's get to that shopping."

CHAPTER 6

SUNDAY WAS CHAD'S DAY to make up for the hours he'd taken off to help with Mary Alice's class earlier in the week. He'd barely been home two minutes before the bell rang, signaling her arrival. Maybe they'd call in an order to Dinner Belles before they got going on decorating his tree. He tugged open the door and stared at the bright green casserole carrier and pie Mary Alice was holding. She had one of those reusable fabric grocery bags thrown over one shoulder. It was bulging.

"You cooked."

"Well, you had to work half the day, so I thought you could do with some home-cooked sustenance to fuel the tree trimming."

"What is it?"

"Poppyseed chicken—my grandmother's recipe—and pecan pie. Which is superior to PEE-CAN pie." She winked at him as she stepped into the house.

A casserole and pie. He'd seen so many of them since moving here, but none had made him smile like this. Or maybe that was just Mary Alice. "You're wearing elf ears." More properly, she was wearing an elf hat with ears attached. It was adorable. She was adorable.

"It seemed appropriately festive for the occasion."

"You make a really good elf." Although, with her creamy skin and bright blue eyes, she was a bit more Middle Earth than North Pole. "What's in the bag?"

"This and that. Fixin's for hot chocolate. A pie server, since I didn't know whether you had one. A few other things."

He led her back to his kitchen, stripping out of his coat and watching as she moved easily around, switching the oven on and pulling more stuff from the bag. A bottle of wine. A corkscrew. A bag of mini marshmallows. Flowers? And were those cloth napkins?

"Is there vanilla ice cream in that magic bag of yours?"

"Well, duh." She pulled out a pint of Blue Bell and stuck it in the freezer. "Pecan pie without ice cream is just sad. How was your day?"

"Not too bad."

While he talked, Mary Alice opened his cabinets until she unearthed a tall glass. Fascinated, he watched as she filled it with water and set to snipping flower stems to make an arrangement for his kitchen table. There was something unreasonably sexy about a woman arranging flowers. Or maybe it was just this woman. Those slim-fingered, competent hands were so graceful. She pulled out plates and silverware, quickly and efficiently setting two places, before sliding the casserole in the oven.

She looked…good in his kitchen. He was probably going to some feminist hell for thinking it. But seeing her there, with her Pyrex dish and pie and the other cheery little touches most people would never have even thought of, he realized how much the house he'd lived in for almost a year didn't feel like a home. Until now. The thought struck him like a fist in the chest.

"I cooked it this morning, so it just has to warm through. I wasn't sure how hungry you were. I figured we could throw it in the oven on low and maybe get the lights on the tree while it's warming up."

Chad barely heard her. She'd walked in with her bag and her casserole and made the place feel inviting in five minutes. He could absolutely imagine coming home to this every night.

Too fast, pal.

But he couldn't shake the image or the way it stirred him.

"Or, I guess, if you're hungry already, we could start with dessert first."

He crossed the space in two strides, knocking the elf hat off as he threaded his hands in her hair and laid his lips over hers. Chad meant to keep the kiss soft and easy, but her instant acquiescence, the way she just melted into him, had him diving deeper. He caged her against the counter and devoured her mouth. Her jolt of surprise had some dim corner of his brain shouting at him to get a leash on this. In just a minute... Then her hands speared into his hair, and she made a needy little whimper that had him going hard. Her mouth opened under his, another potent surrender, and he was lost.

He lifted her onto the counter, stepping between the V of her thighs and dragging her forward, until her center was pressed against the erection his scrubs did nothing to hide. She wrapped her legs around his waist and wriggled closer. Whatever blood had been left in his brain drained south. Yes, God, yes, he wanted her. Warm and willing and his.

His hands skated under her sweater, finding soft, warm skin and lace. Her breasts filled his palms, the nipples pearling under his touch. He traced them, loving the way she arched in a wordless demand for more. He wanted to see, wanted to taste, so he tugged the sweater up. Mary Alice's hands slid under his scrub top, nails scraping down his back as she tightened her legs to bring them even closer.

Something rolled off the counter and hit the floor with a clatter. The sound had him jolting, snapping him out of the moment and allowing him to find a thread of control. He was on the verge of taking Mary Alice in the middle of his kitchen.

Appalled at his behavior, he removed his hands from her breasts and broke the kiss. "I'm sorry. I—"

Her fingers pressed against his lips. "Unless the next words to fall out of your mouth are 'I have to stop' or some variation of 'I think this is a mistake,' then you have nothing to apologize for." She was breathless, her lips swollen from his, and he just wanted to dive right back in.

"I don't usually have such little control."

The smile that curved her lips could only be described as feline. "I like it."

He blinked at her.

"I'm an elementary school teacher, Chad, not a saint." She leaned up to press a kiss to the underside of his jaw. "So, let me use small words and short sentences that even my students couldn't misunderstand: I want this. I want you."

God bless enthusiastic consent. Christmas was apparently coming early this year. "Thank God." She twined her arms around his neck, pulling him back, but Chad shook his head. "Not here." She deserved more than a quickie in the kitchen. Boosting her up, he carried her down the hall to his bedroom. He didn't know what state it was in and didn't care. He arrowed straight for the bed and followed her down onto it.

"Now, where were we?"

"Now, where were we?"

Mary Alice couldn't see more than the outline of Chad's face in the dark, but she could hear the smile in his voice, and even if she hadn't, there was no doubt he was on board. Thank God. The weight of him pressed her into the mattress and felt glorious.

For one moment, she hesitated. Was this a mistake? Was it too soon? She'd done her best to shut this part of herself off the last few months. Now that he'd opened the door, it was as if every erotic thought and desire she'd repressed was flooding out. She wanted to touch and take and be taken. And she wanted Chad to be the one to do it.

Tipping her face to his, she found his mouth, giving him a little nip. "We are both wearing way too many clothes."

"In a hurry?"

"Yes." She didn't know why. She hadn't even been planning on this tonight. But then he'd kissed her and his control had slipped. The sweetness she'd come to expect from him gave way to heat—so much heat. She'd had the barest taste of it that first time he'd kissed her. Since then he'd been so carefully controlled, as if he thought she'd spook. Until tonight, when he just couldn't rein it in. And she'd loved it. Loved the idea that she could inspire that. She wanted to make him lose control completely.

Chad shoved himself up, tugging off his scrub top with one hand, even as she wrestled off her sweater.

Her hands met bare flesh, racing over his chest and finding a helluva lot more definition and muscle than she'd expected. "Where do you find time to build this?" She followed her hands with her lips, wresting a groan from him as he answered.

"I have a home gym."

"You make really good use of it." She wanted

to see him. But later. Right now, she wanted to map the contours of that chest with her mouth.

Before she could start, he scooted down her body, kissing along her throat and collar bone, moving lower, to her breasts, and cupping them in his hands again. Mary Alice bowed up, pressing into his palms, needing more contact. "Still with the too many clothes."

"Can't have that," he murmured.

Reaching behind her back, he flicked open the clasp of her bra and drew it away. Then his mouth was on her, warm and sure as he licked and sucked her sensitive nipples. Mary Alice dropped her head back on a moan, feeling a lovely, liquid heat pool between her thighs with every tug of his lips. "Mmm, more."

Cool air met her heated skin as he unzipped her jeans, tugging them down, along with her underwear. "I have a confession."

She tensed. "About?"

"I've totally got 'Hot for Teacher' playing in the back of my head."

Laughing, she relaxed. "I'm shattering stereotypes all over the place."

"In all the best possible ways." He came back to her, his hands skimming up her bare legs, and she said a prayer of thanks she'd shaved this morning. "You have really amazing legs."

"I run," she managed, as he made it past her knees, stroking slowly up the inside of her thighs.

"Me, too. We should do that sometime."

"That is not at all what I'm interested in doing at the moment."

Bent over her, he chuckled, pressing a kiss to her hip, sliding his hands higher, his thumbs tantalizingly close to where she wanted him to touch her and yet much too far away. Restless, impatient and so very, very needy, she groaned his name in frustration.

Nudging her legs apart to make room for his shoulders, he settled between them. "Is this what you want?" He blew gently, his warm breath making her clench and shudder.

"God yes."

He used his fingers to part her and pressed his mouth to her center. Sensation crashed through her. Every inch of her body tightened against the onslaught, as he battered her with wave after wave of pleasure, until she was helpless to do anything but ride the current. She was drowning, gasping for air, gasping his name as he dragged her up and over a brutal peak. Then everything went lax. The calm after the storm. Or maybe it was only the eye.

Lazily, Chad stroked her hip and pressed a kiss to the quivering muscles of her thighs. "Better?" He sounded smug and self-satisfied. Under other circumstances, that might have been annoying, but who was she to complain after an orgasm like that?

"Jesus. And here I thought surgeons were supposed to be talented with their *hands*."

"Oh, we are. Need a demonstration?"

Mary Alice found the strength to crack an eye open and peer down her body at him. "That wasn't a challenge."

He took it as one anyway. Only when he'd

rendered her mindless and shot her over the edge a second time did he strip out of the rest of the scrubs and reach for the bedside table. She heard the crackle of a condom being ripped open, then he rose over her, settling into the cradle of her hips. "You okay?"

"I will be in just a..." She shifted until the blunt head of him nudged her entrance, making already sensitive nerve endings sing. "There."

He murmured her name as he pressed just barely inside her, a welcome answer to the ache at her core. Wanting more, she arched up, wrapping her legs around his hips as he slowly rocked into her, inch by gradual inch.

"Better," she gasped. "Much...much...oh God, there."

He filled her up with more than simply his body. As he held still, giving her a chance to adjust, he kissed her, long and deep, with something that was more than sweetness, more than heat. It was that elusive something she chased as he began to move, driving her up a third time. As the storm of pleasure overtook them both, she clung to the sensation and to him. Only as she lay tangled and sweaty against him did she recognize it for what the feeling was.

He made her feel cherished. The focus of his world—at least for right now.

"YOU WERE one of those kids who took your time opening Christmas presents instead of ripping off the paper, weren't you?" Mary Alice's sleepy voice held a thread of accusation.

Stroking a hand down the smooth skin of her back, Chad smiled and kissed her. "I learned the value of building anticipation early."

"Boy, did you." She stretched against him, and he loved every gloriously naked inch. "I feel amazing."

"I feel pretty damned amazing myself. Happy and sated. For now." Gently, he bit down on her shoulder.

"Mmm. I'm already looking forward to next

time."

"I'm gonna need fuel to manage a next time."

"Fuel." She sat bolt upright in bed. "The casserole!" With a bounce, she leapt out of bed and raced naked from the room.

God, what a woman.

Slipping on his boxers, Chad grabbed one of his shirts from the closet and headed into the kitchen. Mary Alice was bent over, pulling the casserole out of the oven. He took a moment to admire her bare ass and felt himself beginning to stir. "Well, that might just inspire me to wait on dinner."

She set the dish on the stove with a thunk and a sigh. "Burned."

Crossing to her, he slipped the shirt around her shoulders. "I'm sorry. Well, I'm not sorry we were otherwise occupied, but I am sorry the dinner you made got ruined."

She shoved her arms into the sleeves. "At least there's still pie."

"Pie is always a good idea."

Mary Alice cut two enormous slices,

warming them in the microwave and adding a generous scoop of vanilla ice cream to the top. They ate at the pretty table she'd set, which was probably for the best, as it hid the tantalizing view of her bare legs. Seeing her in his shirt was temptation enough.

Chad forked up a bite and let the rich sweetness melt on his tongue. "This pie is delicious."

"I have a question."

"Yes, you can absolutely eat the next slice off my abs, so long as I get quid pro quo."

She paused, the fork halfway to her lips, her mouth falling open, even as her eyes went dark. "Well, God. There's an image."

"Not what you were going to ask?"

"No, but we can file that away for later."

"Sweet."

One quick laugh burst out of her. "No, I wondered what it was that set you off earlier."

"Pretty sure that was you."

That quick, delighted smile was a reward unto itself. "No, I meant in the kitchen, when you kissed me. What was that about?"

They'd just been as intimate as two people could be. Surely, she wouldn't balk at this. "You were standing there, looking gorgeous, asking about my day, with a casserole in the oven. You made my house feel like home, and I was thinking how nice it would be to come home to that every day." He shrugged with more nonchalance than he felt. "Maybe it's unenlightened or sexist of me, but I find the whole idea of coming home to a wife and family incredibly appealing."

"I don't think it's sexist to want marriage and family. It's only sexist if you expect those things to exist solely for your own edification at the expense of your partner's." She took a bite of her own pie and seemed to consider. "That's really what you're after? Long-term? I mean, in general."

"Isn't it what everybody's after in the grand scheme of things?"

"No." The word was flat and matter-of-fact.

Chad cursed himself for the flippant response because that clearly hadn't been what her ex had wanted. At least not with her. So, he ate more pie and gave her question the serious answer it deserved. "I'm thirty-four. Most of the years my friends were getting married, I was buried in school or residency. Some of my classmates married during all of that, but they barely saw their spouses or kids, if they had them. I didn't want that. I grew up with that in my own family. My dad was a virtual stranger, who always put his practice ahead of us."

"I remember you saying your dad was a doctor, too."

"He's a cardio-thoracic surgeon. A brilliant one, who's saved a lot of lives. But he neglected his family to do it. I didn't want to be that guy. It's why I took a position as head of emergency medicine here instead of being a full-time trauma surgeon at a bigger hospital. I wanted time for an actual life. I want to be able to put my eventual wife and family first."

Mary Alice put the fork down. She shifted her gaze to the plate and wiped her mouth with a napkin, but Chad saw the faint tremble of her lip. He set his own fork aside and reached for her hand. "What is it? What did I say wrong?"

She swallowed, and when she met his gaze again, those big baby blues were suspiciously shiny. "Nothing. You didn't say anything wrong. You said everything right, in fact."

He felt a little like he was walking a mine-field. "And that…upsets you?"

She sucked in a breath and looked at the ceiling. "I just spent the last two years taking a backseat to a job and someone else's needs. And I think I'm only just realizing exactly how much I short-changed myself for sticking with it. With him. I deserved better."

Chad hauled her into his lap and wrapped his arms around her. "I'll give you better. As long as you're with me. That's a promise."

She framed his face between her palms and laid her lips over his in a kiss that said *thank you* as much as any words. "You are a very good man, Chad Phillips. And I suppose I'll have to thank Finn for making herself sick as three dogs so we had a chance to meet."

"I'll buy her a dartboard for her very own." He thought about taking her back to bed, making use of the rest of that pie, but he sensed she needed to take things down a notch and do something easy. "Why don't we get started on the tree?"

He knew it was the right move when she slid off his lap and moved back to the seemingly endless bag of surprises. "I brought something for you."

"Yeah? In addition to dinner, dessert, and you? Because I'm not sure even I've been that good this year."

Mary Alice replaced her elf hat, which inspired a whole new set of fantasies, as she stood there, bare-legged and naked beneath his shirt. "I think there's an entirely acceptable level of naughty. But no." She pulled something out and brought it over. "The ornament you made in my class. I know you weren't there the day we painted, so I finished it for you."

The wreath he'd made had turned out really well. She'd run a red ribbon through a hole at the top to hang it and carved the year in the back. He liked that it was something they'd sort of made together. "Well, obviously that should go front and center."

"And—" She went back to the bag and pulled out a zip top bag full of candy canes made of beads. "My class made you these. They had such fun working with you, they wanted to do something for you for Christmas, so we did these on Friday."

Chad found himself absurdly touched that a bunch of third-graders had liked him that much. "That is awesome." He wondered what it would feel like when someday his own kids made ornaments for the tree. Looking at the kitchen table, with their dessert plates and napkins, he could imagine a couple of kids there making macaroni angels and popsicle stick reindeer. Kids with snaggletoothed grins and big blue eyes. Yeah, that was a good dream.

He drew Mary Alice in for another kiss. "I'll get the lights."

CHAPTER 7

SCHOOL WAS OFFICIALLY OUT for Christmas break and not a moment too soon. Donations were pouring in for Fountain of Hope and that meant Mary Alice and her team were about to be exceptionally busy. They had three days to get everything picked up from the donation sites, wrapped, and delivered to each family. She'd appointed herself to swing by the hospital, on the off-chance Chad had a few minutes to grab some coffee.

It seemed ridiculous to miss him. She'd just seen him last night. And while there hadn't been time for a reprisal of Sunday—or execution of his most excellent suggestion of what to do with the last of that pie—she was wearing a turtleneck sweater today to cover up the beard burn on her throat. She, Mary Alice Reed, was dating one of Wishful's most eligible bachelors, and it felt fantastic.

She had a spring in her step as she strode through the automatic doors and headed for the elevator up to the second-floor nurse's station. Corinne had said everything was gathered and stored in a locked closet upstairs. Not too convenient for off-loading, but she'd promised to round up a few pairs of extra hands to help haul everything out to Mary Alice's car. She'd just touch base, then swing by the ER.

Mary Alice took the elevator up, humming to herself. She hadn't planned on having a new boyfriend this close to Christmas, which put her at something of a disadvantage on the gift-giving front. It was hard to know what was appropriate, given the newness of their relationship. Maybe something for his house? He'd seemed to like the idea of homey touches, and certainly he could use some. But that seemed like she was making a claim on his space, and despite the giddy sense that they were definitely headed in that direction, it was way too soon to do that. Maybe something baked. He had really liked the pie.

Flipping through her mental index of recipes, Mary Alice stepped off the elevator and right into a broad chest. "Oh!"

Big, familiar hands came up to cup her shoulders and steady her. "Sorry about that."

Mary Alice's stomach clenched as she looked up—way up—into Judd's familiar blue eyes. "Hey. What are you doing here?" He hated hospitals with a vengeance.

Autumn stepped out from behind him and offered a little wave. "Hi."

Seeing the other woman, Mary Alice expected to feel anger or jealousy—something. But seeing her here, it wasn't any of those emotions at the forefront. It was concern. Autumn had a congenital heart defect. She'd had surgery back in high school and had been under strict medical supervision ever since. No matter what had passed between them, she didn't wish the other woman ill. "Is everything okay?"

Neither of them were throwing off worried vibes. In fact, they both seemed to be trying to repress a bubbling excitement.

Autumn's fair cheeks flushed. "I'm fine. Great, in fact." She shifted, but not before Mary Alice's gaze dropped to the glossy black and white photo in her hand. An ultrasound.

"Oh. Oh! You're...I..." Mary Alice blinked, suddenly a little breathless, as if she'd been sucker punched. "Congratulations." What else was there to say?

"Thanks. It was...a surprise."

For you and me both.

"I'm sure." Despite the fact that her head was reeling and she felt like throwing up, Mary Alice lifted her gaze to Judd and forced a smile. "I'm happy for you. Best to you both. I've got donations to pick up." She started to move past them.

"Mary Alice." Judd's voice had her stopping to look back. "I'm glad about Chad."

"So am I." Then she hurried around the corner and out of sight.

She didn't stop at the nurse's station. Instead, she made for the nearest stairwell, needing to get away from people until she could get herself under control. The door slammed shut behind her with a definitive clang that echoed through the space. And for long minutes, she just stood on the landing, sucking in air and trying not to cry.

Damn it. Damn it, she'd thought she was past this. She'd thought she was more evolved than this. But seeing them like that, looking so damned happy to have what she'd always wanted...it was such a slap in the face. She'd been so, so stupid for refusing to see what was right in front of them both and cutting him loose a long time ago. By the power of her will alone, she'd tried to wish him into being what she wanted him to be—a perfect, devoted, home and family guy. And there was irrefutable proof that he absolutely *was* that guy. But he was someone else's Mr. Home and Family.

She needed to find hers now. And maybe she had. Things with Chad, while new, were so very good. She hoped to God she wasn't blinded by wishful thinking this time.

With a steadying breath, she headed down the stairs. She would let go of the anger and the hurt. Right now, she needed to find Chad. Needed to remind herself that he wasn't some dream she'd woken up from. And she just wanted a hug.

The ER was only partly full when Mary Alice walked in. She scanned the patients, trying to judge how busy they really were and whether she could interrupt for five minutes without causing problems. Even as she started toward the desk, the swinging doors to the back opened and Chad came out.

Her bruised heart lifted at the sight of him. His own face brightened with a blazing smile. But he wasn't looking at her. A gorgeous, leggy brunette raced across the room and launched herself at him on a laugh. Chad caught her close, swinging her around in a circle before setting her back on her Jimmy-Choo-clad feet with a smacking kiss. On the mouth. And even if Mary Alice had been wrong about that, the brunette reached up and ran her fingers through his hair in a gesture that spoke of unquestionable intimacy as she beamed up at him.

Mary Alice stumbled back a step. She didn't know who this woman was, and it wasn't in her to cross over and confront them to find out. Not now. In the end, it didn't matter. Because Mary Alice was done. She'd learned her lesson with Judd. She wasn't about to stay in a relationship with a guy who had any kind of intimate attachment to another woman. That was a deal breaker.

Fool me once, she thought, and headed for the exit.

CHAD WAS STILL RIDING HIGH on Sonya's surprise visit and her good news. He'd hoped for a chance to introduce her to Mary Alice. She was supposed to be stopping by to pick up the donations for Fountain of Hope this afternoon, but he hadn't seen her, and Sonya had to get on down to Jackson for her meeting. But she'd promised to come back through tomorrow and spend a night on her way back to Birmingham. Maybe he could arrange a dinner so Sonya could get a chance to meet the woman he was so crazy about.

During a brief lull late in the afternoon, he headed up to the second-floor nurse's station to find out if anybody had seen Mary Alice. Maybe she'd come through while he was tied up with that dislocated shoulder. Rosemary Newsome, the charge nurse, was reviewing charts at the desk.

"Hey, has Mary Alice been by to pick up the donations yet?"

"Oh, somebody else came by to get them about an hour ago."

"Huh. I thought Mary Alice was coming." Strange that she hadn't texted him to mention she wouldn't be by. "Maybe she got hung up." Chad tapped the counter with his palm and started to turn.

"No, she was here earlier," Corinne said. "I saw her going down the hall. She looked upset."

"Any idea why?"

Corinne shrugged. "Don't know."

"Maybe she ran into her ex. He was up here earlier, round about that same time, I think," Rosemary added. "They had their first ultrasound."

Married six weeks after breakup and now with a baby on the way? Ouch. No wonder she's upset.

"Thanks."

Chad found a quiet corner and tried to call her. Straight to voicemail. "Hey, it's me. Missed you at the hospital this afternoon. I wanted to see if everything was all right. Corinne said you seemed upset when she saw you. Call me back."

He sent a text to check on her, too, but by the end of his shift, he still hadn't gotten an answer. More than a little concerned, he wrapped up his files as quickly as possible and drove straight to her house.

She took long enough to answer the door, he considered circling around to the back to see if it was unlocked. But she did answer eventually, her eyes red-rimmed and puffy, her cheeks still wet with tears. Chad stepped inside, reaching for her. "Honey, what happened?"

Mary Alice flinched back from his touch. "Don't."

He dropped his hands and took a step back, recognizing he was on boggy ground. Clearly something had happened. He put on his clinician's hat automatically trying to diagnose as he said quietly, "Okay. Tell me what's wrong."

"I saw you." Though she didn't raise her voice, the accusation hit him like a slap. So did the fresh tears welling in her eyes.

What was she talking about? "Saw me what?"

"Kissing that other woman."

Sonya. She'd seen him with Sonya. It had

been nothing. A greeting between old friends. But he could imagine how it must have looked to Mary Alice. Now the tears made sense. "It's not what you think. Sonya and I are just friends."

Mary Alice shot him a withering look. "I have guy friends. I don't kiss them like that."

He had to tread very, very carefully here. "There's a lot of history there. We were together for a long time, but—"

"Together?"

"We used to be engaged. But it's ancient history."

"Engaged. You're still friends with a woman you were going to marry? *The* woman who broke things off with you only two months before you walked down the aisle," she corrected, clearly putting two and two together.

"Yeah. It's complicated." Probably, he should have told her this story already, but he hadn't expected them to be meeting any time soon, and who really wanted to talk about their ex early in a new relationship?

Mary Alice shook her head. "I can't do this. I'm sorry, I just can't. Not again."

She was taking that two and two and getting six. "It's not what you think," he repeated. "Just let me explain."

"I don't want your explanation, Chad. I don't care. I just spent two years having explanations shoved down my throat about how I didn't need to worry, that Judd and Autumn were just friends, nothing more. And now they're married with a baby on the way."

So she had found out Autumn was pregnant when she came to the hospital earlier. Chad knew how much Mary Alice wanted a family, how she'd expected that when she'd invested all that time and effort into Judd. He kept his voice gentle. "I can see how that would be upsetting. And if you came to find me after finding that out, I can see how you'd take what you saw with me and Sonya the wrong way, but I'm not Judd."

"No, you're not. But you remember that conversation we had about deal breakers? This is one of mine. I can't be with a guy with close female friends. I'm not foolish enough to put myself in a position to go through all this again."

Temper and frustration began to simmer. She was hell-bound and determined that he'd put her through the same kind of heartbreak. Didn't she understand how he felt about her?

Obviously not.

They hadn't had enough time together for him to overcome the two years of disappointment. He'd had twelve years to get past his shit from his breakup with Sonya. Mary Alice hadn't even had twelve months. So, he made the effort to bank the temper, to try and find the words she needed.

"Mary Alice, please, just let me explain."

Arms crossed over her middle, she just shook her head. "I can't do this. I just can't. Please go."

He wanted to fight her. He wanted to hold her and wipe away those tears she was trying so damned hard not to shed. She wasn't going to listen. Not tonight, anyway.

It went against every instinct, but he acquiesced. "All right. But come find me when you're ready to talk."

"I've said everything I have to say."

"I haven't." Though he wanted to slam it, he shut the door quietly behind him and went in search of a beer.

CHAPTER 8

"WHERE'S DR. MCHOTTIE?" PRESLEY teased. "I figured he'd be here for this, since you two have been joined at the hip the last few weeks."

The stunning pain of betrayal ripped through Mary Alice again, and her hands stilled on the box she'd yet to finish wrapping. "I don't want to talk about it." Certainly not here in the community center gym, where more than a dozen volunteers were set up at wrapping stations within earshot.

Her friends instantly sobered and ex-changed a look.

Margot stepped closer, lowered her voice. "What happened?"

Mary Alice just shook her head as a fresh bout of tears built in her throat. She was so tired of crying over guys. Maybe she'd just get a dog. That seemed more on par with the kind of emotional investment she was prepared to make these days. At least a dog would love her unconditionally.

Margot turned and waved. "Hey Liza? Can you and Mamie come finish this batch up? We're gonna go take stock of how much we have left to wrap."

Without waiting for assent, she hustled Mary Alice out of the gym and down the hall to the smaller room being used to store donations. As soon as Presley and Finn trailed them inside, Margot shut the door and locked it. "Spill."

"Does this have something to do with the fact that you sent someone else to get donations from the hospital yesterday?" Presley asked.

Mary Alice pinched the bridge of her nose and swallowed against the lump in her throat. "I went myself, like I planned. But I wanted to see Chad before we loaded everything up because I was upset, and I just needed…Well, it doesn't matter what I needed. I saw him kissing another woman."

"That bastard!" Finn exploded.

"Wait," Margot interrupted. "You were upset before you went to see him? Why? Did he do something else?"

"No, that wasn't anything to do with him at all." She heaved a sigh. "I ran into Judd and Autumn."

"Were they ugly to you?" Presley asked.

"No, of course not." Mary Alice lifted her head to look at her friends. "She's pregnant."

Their shocked silence was absolute and weighty.

"Oh honey." Margot wrapped her in a hug. "No wonder you were upset."

"How far along?" Presley asked gently. "I

mean, with the timing and...are you worried they were...together before you broke up?"

"No." Of all the accusations she might have leveled at Judd, she knew without a shred of doubt that he'd never cheated on her. "Probably eight weeks. Everything's on the up and up there. It was just such a shock, and I thought, thank God I'm with someone now who's on the same page."

"So, you went to find Chad for comfort," Margot concluded.

Mary Alice nodded. "And then there he was."

"He was just in the ER making out with some chick?" Finn asked in disgust.

"Well, no. That would be hideously unprofessional."

"Tell us exactly what happened," Presley ordered.

Mary Alice spelled it out. Easy enough to do, since the whole thing was burned into her brain.

"Did you confront him?" Finn demanded.

"No. Not then. I left. He came over after he got off work."

"And what did he have to say for himself?"

Mary Alice shrugged. "What any guy caught would say. 'It's not what you think.'"

"Then what was it?" Margot asked.

"He claimed they're just friends. There's long history there, but oh, their engagement was forever ago."

"He's kissing on an ex fiancée?" Presley cocked a disbelieving brow.

"That's what I said. He just told me it was complicated and that he could explain."

Margot leaned back against a table. "What was his explanation?"

"I don't know. I asked him to go."

"Wait, so you didn't let him explain?" Presley asked.

"I don't care what his explanation is. I spent two years hearing explanations from Judd about how Autumn was no threat. I'm not about to stay in a relationship with another guy who's got some kind of deep ties to another woman he claims is only a friend. I'm not going through that again."

"You should talk to him," Finn said.

Mary Alice stared at her. "This coming from *you?* I figured you'd be at the head of the lynch mob."

"If he needs it, I will be. But I'm just saying, give him a chance to explain."

"Why?"

"Because down the road, the not knowing will drive you nuts. Trust me on this. Even if it's bullshit, it's better to hear the explanation than to wonder."

"I agree," Margot said. "Though I'm not so sure whatever his explanation is will be bullshit."

"Are you kidding me?" Mary Alice demanded.

"Hear me out. One of your biggest issues with Judd is the fact that he didn't put you first. Chad's different. He seems more than willing to juggle his job and whatever else he has to in order to spend time with you. He's thoughtful and has put you first wherever he can. And there's none of that sense of guilt and obligation that became so much a part of your relationship with Judd. At the very least, you owe him a chance to make that explanation. Because he's not Judd, and I don't think it's fair of you to treat him like he is."

She opened her mouth to argue.

"We're not saying you have to take him back," Presley told her. "And we're not saying you don't have a right to be upset. But I think your whole reaction to the situation was entirely colored by being upset over Judd and Autumn. Which is understandable. You're gun-shy after all that. But everything you've told us about Chad up to now indicates he's a good guy, who's really into you. And you're really into him. Do you really want to risk letting that go when you might have made a mistake?"

They made some valid points. But what if she heard him out and his explanation swayed her into giving him another chance and doing exactly what she'd done with Judd? She absolutely couldn't go through that again.

Needing something to do with her hands, Mary Alice turned away and grabbed the nearest box of donations. She checked the tag, her hands stilling as she saw Isaiah's name. Her heart squeezed, remembering the day she and Chad had spent together shopping for him and the others. Aware of her friends' eyes on her, she said nothing, lifting the contents out of the box. She paused at the toy medical kit she found inside. This hadn't been part of what they'd bought in Lawley. Beneath the bag, she found a child-sized lab coat and a real stethoscope, with a note attached. *You'll need it one day for med school.*

How could she reconcile the man who would do this for a child, the man who would go to all the trouble to design a personalized scavenger hunt around her favorite Christmas movie, the man who'd made love to her so thoroughly, with the guy she was accusing him of being? How could she let one thing outweigh the balance of all the kindness she'd seen from him?

Head bent as fresh tears slid down her cheeks, Mary Alice gripped the edge of the box. "God help me."

CHAD GOT HOME from work late and opened the door to the scent of food and the sound of music pumping out of his kitchen. Heart thumping, he hurried into the kitchen.

Sonya turned from the counter, a broad smile on her beautiful face. "Hey handsome. I got Chinese. Thanks for telling me where the spare key was hidden."

Chad called himself an idiot. He'd seen Sonya's car outside, knew it wasn't Mary Alice waiting for him. But still, a part of him had hoped she'd had a change of heart. His keen disappointment was definitive proof that it wasn't just any woman with dinner he wanted to come home to, it was that particular woman.

"Oh, I know that face. Bad day? Did you lose someone at work?" Sonya asked gently.

Chad moved past her to the fridge. "Not the way you mean." He popped the top on a Yuengling and tipped it back.

"Is your lady too tied up to come meet me? Is that what's got you in a shitty mood?"

Heading into the living room, he dropped onto the sofa and leaned his head back. "She's not my lady. Not anymore." Admitting that left a bitter taste in his mouth that the beer did nothing to assuage.

Sonya folded herself gracefully onto the other end of the couch. "What happened?"

His lips curved, though he certainly saw no humor in the situation. "She saw me with you."

"What? But that was nothing."

"She doesn't think so. She wouldn't let me explain."

"That's not very sporting of her. I'm not sure she's worth all the praise you heaped on her if she can't be bothered to listen."

Chad growled. "She has her reasons." He

didn't have to like them, but he recognized they were very real for her.

Sonya arched one perfectly-shaped brow. "Well, I'm starved. How about we load up our plates, and you tell me what they are so I can help you figure out how to fix this? I got all your favorites."

She'd come all this way to see him. The least he could do was humor her. Chad dragged his ass off the sofa and filled his plate with sweet and sour pork, crab rangoon, and egg rolls. He carried it all back into the living room, along with the pint of fried rice, and began to shovel in food as he sketched out the particulars of what he knew about Mary Alice's relationship with Judd.

"I know the guy a little. I've treated his wife. The two of them are so obviously exactly right for each other. Like long-history, finish each other's sentences, two halves of one whole kind of perfect. I cannot imagine what the hell Judd was doing with Mary Alice in the first place. And I don't know how she managed to delude herself about it for so long."

"You managed to delude yourself about me. If I hadn't gotten up the courage to confess, and we'd gone through with the wedding, who knows where we'd be right now."

Chad thought about that last year and about the hard truth Sonya had forced him to face. "Love is blind."

"Yeah. Do you think she's still in love with him?"

"No. I don't think she'd have been with me if she were. She knows she's better off without him, that she deserves so much more than he gave her. But I don't think her heart has a hundred percent caught up with her head on the subject of Judd. She ran into the pair of them at the hospital yesterday and found out Autumn's pregnant, right before she saw us."

Sonya cringed. "Ouch. In love with him or not, that's gotta hurt. I think it always feels weird when you see your ex moving on with someone else and doing the things you thought you'd be doing with them."

Chad gave her a wry smile. "Yeah, I'm aware."

Sonya patted his knee. "But you got over me. I concede that, under the circumstances, what she saw looked bad. But you and I both know that our situation isn't what she thinks. Even if I were free, we are *never* going to reconcile."

"I love these visits. You really know how to make a guy feel wanted."

"You know I love you. But you're not equipped to handle me, and we both know it."

Chad groaned.

"If she's half the woman you say she is, she's bound to get past that first wave of hurt to listen to you."

Looking over at the Christmas tree he wouldn't even have without Mary Alice, he remembered her tears and the look of absolute betrayal in her eyes. It made his gut clench that he'd hurt her, even inadvertently. "That may be a while."

"You're a patient guy. If she's worth it, you'll wait. And if she's not, you'll find someone else."

"I don't want someone else. I want her. It's fast and maybe kind of unreasonable, but I'm crazy about her. She just slipped right into the life I've built here, and everything came into focus. I can see my life with her—next week, next year, in twenty years. Marriage. Kids. The whole shebang."

"That certainly seems serious. You haven't had that kind of long-term view about a woman since—"

"You," he finished.

"You're in love with her."

He scrubbed both hands over his face. "Shit. Yeah, I am."

Sonya sighed and tipped back her own beer. "Chad, you know I love you. I want you to find what I've found. And if that's really what you've got with Mary Alice, then I want to do anything I can to help you save it."

"I appreciate the thought. But I don't know that there's anything you can do. You trying to talk to her would probably only make everything worse. She's just got to work her way around to it on her own." Who knew how long that would take?

"Well, at least it's just about Christmas. You'll be headed home in a few days, right?"

"Not until day after. I'm on-call at the hospital Christmas Eve and Christmas Day. I wanted to give the rest of my staff a chance to be with their families. A bunch of them have kids."

Sonya shot him an affectionate smile. "There's that generous guy I love. Will you be seeing her again before then because of this charity of hers? What was it?"

"Fountain of Hope. I don't know. Delivery day is Saturday. I'm signed up to help with that, but I figure she'll arrange everything so she doesn't actually have to see me." He hated that. Mary Alice had told him how much she loved the delivery part of the process. "Maybe I should back out."

"Absolutely not," Sonya insisted. "You show up and you be the same great guy you've been since day one. Remind her what she's missing and that you're still here."

"I don't want to put pressure on her."

"It's not putting pressure to be yourself and follow through on your commitments. It sounds like her ex wasn't great at that. Give her a glimpse of what she's giving up. Besides, it's all about holiday spirit and goodwill, right?"

He really did want to follow the project through to the end. "All right." As they argued over the last egg roll, he wondered if holiday spirit and goodwill would be enough.

CHAPTER 9

MARY ALICE WAS GOING to be late for D-Day. But she was hoping to see Chad today and get a chance to talk to him. After how she'd reacted, she felt like she needed a little extra insurance, so here she was at the fountain. How many times in her life had she walked by it? Countless. She'd stopped before, had lunch perched on its ledge, but she'd never wished. Maybe because it had been hard to believe when the fountain was all but defunct, with barely a trickle of water dribbling down. But it seemed, over the past couple of years, it had come back to life.

Ridiculous. They'd probably just finally figured out what was wrong and fixed it. But there was no denying the appeal of the steady burble of water. Some kind of heaters in the basin kept the water from freezing during the cold winter nights. Through the clear water, she could see hundreds of glittering coins. Maybe more. And she was about to add her own. As soon as she figured out exactly what to wish for.

For Chad to show up today? He'd signed up before her blow up, but he didn't strike her as the kind of guy who'd back out on a commitment just because of that. Fountain of Hope had become important to him. So, she'd bank on that. Should she wish for his explanation to be reasonable? That seemed a waste. Wishing wasn't likely to change the truth, whatever it was. No, what she really needed was a dose of personal fortitude to get through it.

I wish for the courage to really hear what Chad has to say.

She let the quarter fly, watching as it arced neatly into the water. Too late, she wondered if she should've wished he'd actually talk to her. But he'd said to come find him when she was ready to talk. Hopefully he hadn't changed his mind on that in the last three days.

The community center was packed when she arrived. She didn't see Chad. Quashing the disappointment, she let loose a two-fingered whistle to get everyone's attention.

"Thank you all for coming to help out on delivery day. Thanks to everyone's hard work, we have an unprecedented number of gifts to deliver today. Every single child was adopted by someone this year."

The group cheered.

"Now, we've made arrangements with the parents or guardians of each child to meet somewhere other than home, in order to maintain secrecy from the kids and privacy for the families. Each delivery will be made in a pair, and most of you have more than one delivery to make. For those of you who are new to the process, I've paired you with someone who was here before."

As Mary Alice read through the list and each couple came up to get their boxes of wrapped presents and meeting locations, she kept an eye on the door. Still no Chad.

He probably got called in for surgery or something.

It was fine. She'd take care of her deliveries and find him later. This had to be taken care of first.

Mary Alice checked her list for the next pair of names. "Cam and Norah Crawford, y'all have three."

Two male feet stepped into her line of vision, and she looked up, expecting to see Cam. But it was Chad, hands shoved in his pockets, face scruffy, hair wind-blown, looking good enough to eat.

Mary Alice wanted nothing more than to frame that face and kiss him. God, how could she have missed him this much in just a matter of days? "Hey."

"Hey."

Aware there were still more than a dozen assignments to pass out, she said, "You're with me today."

After a long, unreadable look, Chad nodded and stepped out of the way.

Once the last of the boxes were passed out and the assorted Fountain of Hope elves scattered to their respective meeting locations, Mary Alice finally turned toward where he waited beside their gifts. There were so many things she wanted to say. To address the white elephant standing between them. But they were on a schedule, and they'd need—she hoped—more time to talk uninterrupted.

"Thanks for coming today."

"I said I would."

Mary Alice felt the silent rebuke. He'd never lied to her, never broken a promise. "Look, I wasn't fair to you, and I'm sorry for it. I owe you a lot more than an apology, and I hope you'll give me the chance for that. But right now, we have places to be. Will you stick around when we're done so we can talk?"

"Sure." He hefted a carton under each arm, leaving one for her. "Lead the way."

They both stayed quiet through their first two deliveries, and it was the first time the silence felt awkward, full of things unsaid. Mary Alice itched to be finished so they could resolve this one way or the other.

"Who's next?" Chad asked.

"Isaiah's grandmother. We're meeting her at the hardware store."

The older woman was waiting when they pulled into the parking lot beside Edison Hardware. Mary Alice parked by her car so they wouldn't have far to transfer the packages. The other woman was already out of the car, beaming by the time Mary Alice and Chad climbed out.

"Della! You're looking wonderful." Mary Alice gently hugged her.

"Thank you, honey, I'm having a good day."

"I'm glad to hear it."

"Seems there's a lot of Christmas going around this week. My doctor called me in on Monday to say my insurance approved a new electronic pain relief doohickey." She lifted the hem of her long skirt to reveal some kind of device strapped to her calf. "I don't have any idea how it works, but I'll just say thank the good Lord that it does. I haven't felt this good in years!"

"It's a Quell. I've read about those," Chad said. "It uses intensive nerve stimulation to activate your body's natural pain blockers."

Della gave him a curious look.

"Chad's a doctor," Mary Alice explained.

"I reckon I'll have to remember that to tell my grandson. He wants to be a doctor himself when he grows up, so he's curious about all kinds of medical stuff."

Mary Alice opened the back hatch. "Well, there are a few things in here that he's going to especially love."

They began offloading packages from one vehicle to the next.

"Will you be okay getting everything inside on your own?" Chad asked.

"I will. It's gonna stay in the trunk until Isaiah's gone to sleep Christmas Eve. He won't go pokin' in there. Then I'll sneak everything in."

Chad pulled out a card and handed it over. "If you need any help, don't hesitate to call. I'm very good at sneaking."

She has no idea, Mary Alice thought, watching Della accept the card and bat her eyes at Chad like a much younger woman.

"Well, thank you, Dr. Phillips."

He smiled. "Just Chad."

They chatted for a few more minutes, before wishing each other a Merry Christmas. Della climbed back in her car, and Mary Alice and Chad watched her drive away.

"Her insurance didn't approve that thing, did it?" Mary Alice asked.

He just shrugged. "It's a small town. I know her doctor."

And that just did it. Mary Alice had fallen into serious like with Chad on their scavenger hunt at Applewhite Farms. She'd fallen into lust in his kitchen. But it was that simple, selfless gesture that would mean so much to a family he didn't even know that had her falling in love with him.

Her stomach pitched and her heart began to race. This wasn't like Judd. That had been a gradual slide, a natural growth of affection over time. This was more like a free fall without a parachute, a prospect made all the more terrifying because she didn't know if he could or would feel the same after how she'd treated him.

Linking her hands together to still the trembling, she lifted her eyes to his. "Can we talk?"

THEY GOT hot cocoa at The Daily Grind—the good kind with whipped cream and a drizzle of chocolate syrup on top—and took it out to the green. Wishful had rolled out its holiday finery weeks ago, and as the sun set, twinkle lights lit up every street lamp, wreath, Christmas tree, and store window. As a rule, Chad loved this time of year. He loved, too, this town he'd decided to call home. But it was impossible not to admit that he loved it more when he was with the woman at his side. The woman who looked vaguely queasy.

"I'm really sorry, Chad. I know I said that already, but it bears repeating." She looked off toward the fountain, both gloved hands wrapped around her to-go cup. "I have prided myself on being so level-headed and well-adjusted about my breakup with Judd. I know, on every logical level, that it was the right thing to do. When he married Autumn, it hurt, but deep down, I wasn't really that surprised. It just confirmed what I'd already known. And I thought, okay, this is it. Nothing can hurt me more than this." She inhaled a breath and looked at him. "Turns out I was wrong."

Chad waited, though he was pretty sure he already knew what she was going to say.

"Running into them that day, finding out

they're pregnant—it was like, 'Hey, you know those things I said I didn't want? Yeah, I lied. I just didn't want them with you.' And that's stupid, because it wasn't like that. Not when we were together, and not after. I'm not still in love with him, and I don't want those things with him anymore. But it just...cut me to the quick because it was right there for me to see, the whole time we were together, and I refused to see it. I felt stupid and hurt, and my first instinct after was to come find you."

He grimaced. "Talk about crap timing." He knew that pain and understood it. "I'm sorry you saw what you saw. I'm sorry I wasn't there when you needed me."

"That's the thing. You knew something was wrong, and you came to find me. And instead of responding to that, I put all my feelings of hurt and grief and betrayal on you and lashed out instead of listening. You didn't deserve that. I'm ready to listen now, if you'll still tell me."

Chad led her over to a bench beneath one of the enormous oaks that dotted the green and pulled her down. He should've told her this story long before now. Still, even after all these years, it was hard to get started. He sipped at his cocoa, giving himself a few extra moments to pull together his thoughts.

"I met Sonya my freshman year of college. We were instant friends, that kind where you meet and in five minutes you've forgotten they weren't always in your life. Our sophomore year, we started dating, and that was just it. We were comfortable together and getting married after we graduated seemed like a foregone conclusion. I asked her to marry me at Thanksgiving our senior year. She said yes, and we started planning the wedding for the following summer. Or, I guess, technically, she did most of the planning, while I was up to my eyeballs in med school applications."

Chad ran a finger along the rim of the cup, remembering. "I should have noticed something was wrong. My head wasn't so far up my ass that I didn't recognize something was off. She was stressed, pulling away some. I just thought it was part of that whole graduation syndrome, where adulthood is barreling toward you like a freight train. So I booked us a trip for spring break. A romantic, mountain cabin getaway, just the two of us. We hadn't slept together at that point. With our respective living arrangements, there hadn't been privacy, and she seemed inclined to wait, which was fine. I didn't take her up there specifically with seduction in mind, but I was twenty-two, so I'd be lying if I said I wasn't hoping."

"I'm sensing things did not go as you anticipated."

"She was twitchy and nervous the whole drive, and I thought maybe she thought I was going to pressure her. So, when we got there—where the cabin owners had set the whole thing up with the honeymoon package of champagne, roses and chocolate—I told her it was fine. We could wait, I just wanted to give her a chance to get away from school and relax. She was chalk white by that point and said she had something she needed to tell me. Pulled me over to the sofa and held both my hands. I was starting to really freak out by that point. I started thinking maybe she was sick, and in the back of my head, I was already trying to diagnose her even before she started to speak."

Mary Alice's hand covered his, and Chad turned his palm up to link his fingers with hers.

"She said she hadn't been honest with me. So then I'm wondering if she's about to say she's cheated on me. If maybe she was pregnant. Then she told me it was hard to be honest with me, when she hadn't been honest with herself. And I had no idea where that was going, so I just sat there and said 'Okay,' knowing that whatever she said was going to change everything."

He could still see her stricken face.

"Had she fallen for someone else?" Mary Alice asked quietly.

"In a manner of speaking." He shifted to look at her. "She'd realized she was gay."

"Oh!"

"I wasn't expecting that either. I asked if she

was sure or if maybe she swung both ways. But no. She loved me, but she couldn't marry me knowing we'd never be what we ought to be together."

"Wow."

"Yeah. The whole thing didn't do much for my ego at the time."

"Were you angry?"

"No. Shocked, sure. Upset, of course. But it's not like that kind of thing is a choice. She couldn't change who she was any more than I can change the fact that I'm left-handed. There wasn't any sense in being angry. Not that that stopped her parents, when she came out to them."

"They didn't take it well?"

"Not even a little bit. They were hateful. Hurtful. They didn't stand by her."

"So, you did," Mary Alice concluded.

"I did. No matter that we weren't getting married, she was my best friend, and I love her. I say that in present tense because I do. I always will. But she's not a threat to you and me."

Mary Alice looked down at their clasped hands and nodded. "It wasn't fair of me to judge you by the yardstick of my past experiences. You're thoughtful, considerate, and I feel amazing when I'm with you. You made me a priority, and you personally have never given me reason to doubt you. I should have listened when you came to me." She lifted her gaze. "If you're willing to give me another shot, I'm all in for trying this with you and *just* you, not you and a ghost from my past."

Chad felt the tension he'd been carrying for days leech out, but he held back the smile. "That depends."

"On what?"

"What are you doing in June?"

"June? I have no idea. Why?"

"I'm gonna need a plus one to Sonya's wedding. That's what she came here to tell me. She's getting married."

Mary Alice's eyes went wide. "Seriously?"

"Yep. I'm gonna be her best man."

She rubbed at her temples and winced. "Wow. I feel *really* stupid now."

Chad wrapped an arm around her. "Let's just call it lessons learned. And hey, we've both finally gotten out the stories of our exes, so there shouldn't be any more surprises. Unless you've got some other kind of skeletons in your closet?"

The relieved smile she aimed up at him untangled the rest of the knots. "No other skeletons."

"And I guess we've got our first fight out of the way, too."

"Guess we did." She hesitated. "There's just one thing."

He tensed. "What?"

"When I'm upset, I stress bake."

"Okay." Where was she going with this?

Her lips curved and there was no mistaking the wicked gleam in her eyes as she leaned in close enough to whisper, "I made another pie."

That thought completely eradicated the cold that had started to seep through his jacket. "Do you have anywhere you have to be the rest of the day?"

"I had the rest of it earmarked for making up."

He bent his head to kiss her. "Then let's go get started."

EPILOGUE

ON A GORGEOUS JUNE evening, as the sun sank into the glittering Gulf of Mexico, Sonya Cooke married Gena Bryson in a small, beachside ceremony. Both brides were radiant, but it was the best man who kept Mary Alice's attention. Chad looked positively swoon-worthy in a tux, and his genuine joy for Sonya shone through, as he watched his friend take the vows she'd once thought to make with him.

Life was strange. But it was also very, very good.

In the wake of the wedding, the thirty or so people in attendance followed the brides to the beach party reception. The luau style dinner was eaten, the cake was cut, and the first dance was had. Mary Alice danced with Chad by tiki torch light and thought the night couldn't get more perfect.

"Let's go for a walk," he suggested.

Willing to follow him anywhere, she stepped away from the group. They slid their shoes off and strolled, hand-in-hand down the beach, toes digging into the sand as the tide rolled in. Mary Alice gave a contented sigh. "It was a good day."

"Yes, it was." He looked back toward the reception, where Sonya and Gena were kicking up their heels to Katy Perry. "They look good together. And so damned happy. Sonya deserves that. I just wish her family had relented and come for the wedding."

Mary Alice leaned up to kiss his cheek. "The family who mattered came." She'd come to understand that's what Sonya was to him. And she'd learned to love Sonya in her own right over the past six months.

Chad dropped his shoes and reeled Mary Alice in. "Thanks for that. And thanks for coming with me."

"A wedding in Florida, tacked on to a beach vacation with the guy I love. Why wouldn't I be all over that?"

"It's been a great trip. Know what would make it even better?"

Sliding her hands up and over his shoulders, she pressed close. "I don't think there's anywhere sufficiently private to sneak away for nookie on the beach, and I'm not keen on the idea of sand in...any of those places."

He laughed. "Pity, but no. Going home together."

She arched her brows. "Were you planning on sticking me on a Greyhound bus?"

"No. I mean going home to the same place. Move in with me, Mary Alice. Come home to me."

Her heart kicked into a gallop. "Are you

serious?"

"Sure am. I even got you a key." He reached into his pocket and brought out one of the silly alligator keychains they'd seen all over in gift shops.

Mary Alice stared at it, fisted in his hand. "That's a really big step."

"I love you, and I'm ready to make a really big step. I think you are, too. What do you say?"

They already spent almost every spare minute together and quite a few nights a week. But was she ready to give up her own space? To take that next step in their relationship? To sleep with him every night and wake up with him every morning? She'd never done that with anyone, but she found she wanted to do it with him.

With a smile, she rose to her toes and brushed her lips over his. "I say yes."

"Then I guess you can have your key." He held up his hand, clearly waiting for her to open hers.

She offered her palm and he dropped the

keychain into it. But it wasn't a key threaded on the chain. It was a ring.

Her gaze whipped back to Chad, who grinned at her. "I figure we might as well do it right." Sobering, he dropped to one knee. "I know we haven't been together all that long, but I don't think it takes that long to know when it's right. It's right with us. You're right for me, and I'm a hundred percent, crazy in love with you. I want to build a life and a family with you, and I don't want to wait some pre-scribed amount of time to start. So marry me, Mary Alice. Marry me, and let's start on the rest of forever."

No hesitation, no question. He knew what he wanted, and what he wanted was her. So she didn't hesitate because she knew what she wanted, too, and he was kneeling in front of her.

"Yes!"

Chad surged to his feet and lifted her with a whoop. As he swung her in a circle, Mary Alice went dizzy and giddy from more than just the momentum. From somewhere in the distance, she was sure she heard applause. They both looked back to where everyone from the wedding was cheering.

"She said yes!" he shouted.

Sonya shot him two thumbs up and waved them back to the party. "We have to celebrate!"

She was waiting with more glasses of champagne. "Well, let's see it!"

Mary Alice opened her palm.

"Oh, don't tell me you really went with that goofy alligator."

"It's memorable," Chad protested.

Mary Alice laughed as he plucked it out of her hand and worked the ring off the keychain so he could slide it on her finger.

"What do you think?"

Looking down at the glitter of diamond and the contrast of her fair skin against the tan of his where their fingers were linked, Mary Alice felt her heart swell. "It's right. It's just exactly right. So are you. And your silly keychain."

Smiling, she tipped her mouth up to his.

Choose Your Next Romance

LONG TIME READERS will be delighted to know that I'm finally writing Mitch Campbell's story. The eldest Campbell cousin has been waiting forever for his happily ever after—and it's gonna be a doozy. With all the family drama you would expect. Hop on over to check out *You Were Meant For Me*--a vacation fling, accidental pregnancy romance with a most surprising shero!

Or you can go check out Judd and Autumn's romance, *Make You Feel My Love,* the first book in the Wishing for a Hero spinoff series. This one is my favorite friends-to-lovers story I've ever written, full of all the Wishful wacky we adore, with a slightly darker edge of suspense.

Also included in this volume is a bonus novelette! *Once Upon A New Year's Eve* is the story for anybody who ever had a crush on your big brother's best friend!

ONCE UPON A NEW YEAR'S EVE

A MEET CUTE ROMANCE

Why didn't I just stay home with the Ben and Jerry's? Surely ringing in the New Year with a pint of What A Cluster *is better than* this.

Gemma Forester picked her way across the gravel parking lot, praying she didn't break an ankle, or worse, one of the precious Jimmy Choos she'd scrimped and saved and paid damn near retail for.

I'm going to kill him, she thought. *That's simply all there is to it. Family immunity does not apply. Mom will have to understand.*

The bar door opened before she could reach

for it. A pair of clearly drunk rednecks stumbled out, lips locked, along with a burst of truly craptastic country music. Whoever the bar had hired to play for the night was going to be lucky if they made it out without requiring intervention from Patrick Swayze and Sam Elliott.

Gemma leapt out of the way before the couple could lurch into her. With the door held open, she watched them stagger to a beat up pick-up truck. The guy managed to get the passenger door open, while simultaneously removing his date's bra from her tank top. Gemma couldn't decide whether to be impressed or appalled. She went inside before her suspicion that they weren't going to make it out of the parking lot was confirmed.

The music didn't stop and all attention didn't focus on her, but she noted her fair share of raised eyebrows. She ignored the catcalls and wolf whistles.

"Eat your heart out, boys," she muttered, crossing to the bar.

As a rule, she wasn't opposed to honky tonks. If she was in the mood and dressed for one, she could totally go for some boot scootin'. But she'd been dressed for dinner at Chez Philippe, where she'd been forced to abandon her very pissed off date before the signature golden champagne raspberry sorbet was served. All because her stupid brother was drinking himself under the table over his latest lost love and making enough of an ass of himself that the bartender had liberated his phone and gone straight down his contact list trying to find someone to come pick him up.

And of course *nobody* else *was dumb enough to pick up tonight,* she thought.

It would've served him right if she'd left him to be arrested for public drunkenness. But there was always that niggling doubt that the bartender hadn't been able to take his keys as easily as his phone, and what if he got behind the wheel...? So with profuse apologies, she'd walked out on her date—who she knew damned well was never going to call again—

and taken a cab down here to Red's Roadhouse.

The bar was two-deep in patrons. She'd had half a dozen offers of drinks and a headache from the caterwauling they apparently called music by the time she fought her way through. Red himself—it had to be him—was manning the taps, a towel tucked into the waistband of his jeans. A giant of a man, with carrot-orange hair ringing a bald pate and an enormous fu manchu mustache, he automatically asked for her order without taking his eyes off the glasses he was filling.

"I'll take the drunk idiot you called me about and get him off your hands."

Red shifted his attention to Gemma. His bushy brows rose. "Well now, which one belongs to you?"

"There's more than one?" she asked.

"Got three. One's sleepin' it off under the pool table over there," he nodded to the left.

Peering between the legs of the players,

Gemma could just make out a figure curled into a fetal position. Too small to be Rick.

"One's workin' on soberin' up with some chili cheese fries down at the other end of the bar."

This guy was hunched over a plastic basket, shoveling in bar food as he swayed a little on the stool. Not Rick.

"The other one's up there." Red jerked his chin toward the back of the room behind her.

Turning, Gemma realized it wasn't a live band that was playing so badly. It was a karaoke station set up on a little stage. Beneath the blinking party lights that were making her queasy without any alcohol, a lone performer clutched at the mic stand and wailed out a very explicit, very profane rendition of "Friends in Low Placcs".

"Oh, of *course*, that one's my drunk idiot brother," she said. Heaving a sigh, she turned back to Red. "Do you have his phone? His keys?"

"Sure. One sec."

She waited, her headache ratcheting closer and closer to migraine territory at her brother's toneless screeching, while Red retrieved his stuff.

"Here you go," he said.

Gemma thumbed the phone on, verified it was Rick's. The keys to his truck she recognized. "Thanks for not calling the cops," she said.

"He's not fightin' anybody. Just nursin' a broken heart. Needs to sleep it off."

She was pretty sure he needed a good kick in the ass, and she'd be happy to provide it.

Temper simmering, she pushed away from the bar. As if sensing her precarious mood, the crowd parted before her, giving her a free path to her brother. As she reached him, she did her best to buckle down fury over her wasted night. No need to let loose with the tongue lashing until he was sober enough to remember it. "That's enough," she said in a low voice, plucking the microphone from his hand.

"But I'm not through yet," Rick slurred.

"Oh, I think you are. And if you leave now, maybe Mr. Brooks won't sue you for the butchery you just made of his music." Gemma laid the mic down and slipped her arm around Rick's waist. "Time to go home."

"Can't go home. No car," he mumbled.

"I've got your keys and your phone" she promised urging him off the stage.

"Need my phone," he said. "Need to call Linda back. She broke up with me, ya know."

"I heard that somewhere," she said. He staggered on the single step and nearly took them both down. Good God, had he *ever* been this drunk before? Surely no woman was worth this.

"Need to talk her out of it," said Rick.

"You need to get home and sleep it off," said Gemma. "C'mon. Siblings don't let siblings drink and dial."

Red's was jumping. A wave of sound broke over Aaron as he stepped into the bar, reminding him why he'd been home alone playing *Call of Duty* instead of out celebrating. He'd ignored Rick's call initially, assuming his buddy was intent on dragging him out as a last minute date for some friend of Linda's. On a break between missions, his curiosity had gotten the better of him, and he'd checked his messages. If Rick was drunk enough that the bartender had confiscated his phone and started looking for somebody to come ride herd on him, something had gone horribly wrong. Aaron suspected that meant Rick had been dumped. One night of getting shit-faced had always been his go-to coping mechanism for that eventuality in college. Not the kind of behavior one expected from an honors student or from the respected attorney he'd grown up to be, but everybody had their flaws. A friend in legitimate need could drag Aaron out where nothing else could.

Too many damned people, Aaron thought, weaving his way toward the bar. As soon as he made it through, he set his curled fists on the bar, claiming a foot of space and struggling not to shove for more. He'd be out of here soon enough. Bodies jostled against his as he waited. And waited, scanning the crowd, looking for Rick. But there were too many faces, too little light.

"What can I getcha?"

"Somebody who works up here left me a voicemail from my buddy's phone, looking for somebody to come get him."

The enormous bartender nodded down to one end of the bar. "That him?"

Aaron followed his gaze, didn't see Rick. "Nope."

"Must be the other one then. His sister's already taking care of things." He gestured with a glass.

Aaron turned toward the back of the bar and stopped dead at first sight of the goddess with her arm around his friend in front the stage.

Hooo-ly shit.

Little Gemma Forester was all grown up.

Aaron clearly remembered the teenage girl. The first time he'd met Gemma, he'd all but swallowed his tongue. It was so absolutely wrong for a fifteen-year-old girl to be that smoking hot, and even more wrong that he couldn't seem to stop himself from noticing. She was fearless and brilliant, having no qualms about jumping into debate with her über-intellectual brother and no problems keeping up. That'd made it hard to remember the age gap, hard to remember that she was completely off-limits for reasons beyond being his best friend's sister. How many high school sophomores could intelligently argue Kafka one minute and political theory as applied to the Empire in *Star Wars* the next? He'd liked her. She was unapologetically direct, without a bashful cell in her body. Unlike so many other girls, she maintained eye contact, pinning him with her icy gray gaze in a way that he found both unnerving and sexy as hell. Confidence always worked for him.

She'd crushed on him as, he imagined, most little sisters did on their older brothers' friends. Trying out her skill at flirtation on him. It had been sweet and flattering. And totally inappropriate.

But this was no teenager. It was one thing to intellectually know that ten years had passed. It was quite another to see evidence of it. From the smooth, dark sweep of her hair, to the well-cut overcoat and fancy shoes that added to her already impressive height, every inch screamed polish and sophistication. And irritation. No wonder. She'd clearly been dragged from a date. Rick wrapped his arms around her, tipping his head against her shoulder and saying something Aaron couldn't make out. Gemma staggered a couple of steps under his weight before finding her footing again.

Aaron shoved away from the bar and went to offer his assistance. The entire population of occupants inside Red's seemed determined to foil that plan. He got bumped, shoved, and even whirled into an impromptu two step by one

187

ambitious blonde that wouldn't take no for an answer. By the time he made it through the pack, Gemma was already heading for the door, Rick suspended between her and a beefy guy in boots and flannel.

Aaron edged in front of them. "Hello Gemma."

"Hello Gemma."

She stopped mid-step and her focus narrowed on blue eyes she hadn't seen in a decade but remembered like it was yesterday.

In all the honky tonks, in all the towns, in all the South, you had to walk into this one.

She actually felt all the maturity, all the layers of poise and composure she'd worked for slip away as nerves began to dance a rumba in her belly and her tongue tied itself in knots. Just like that, she was fifteen again, with a crush on her brother's best friend. A crush that got totally shot down.

Aaron Hendricks smiled at her, flashing that slightly crooked incisor and she felt a blast of very adult heat blow through her system, complicating the nerves with a healthy dose of pure chemistry that scrambled her brain. *Oh. My. God.*

"Aaron," she said. Her voice came out breathless. Mortification flared bright. She could feel the color rising in her cheeks and hoped the lousy lighting was low enough to hide it. The need to escape beat in her blood. No. No, she couldn't deal with this, couldn't deal with *him.*

"What are you doing here?" she managed, tightening her grip on Rick, who was only semi-conscious by now.

"I think Red went through Rick's entire contact list. I got the voicemail, so I came to get him."

Because Aaron was still the dedicated, *responsible* friend in the bunch. She'd always liked that about him.

"I'm taking him home," she said. Under

other circumstances, she might've cringed at the brusque, dismissive tone. She wasn't rude, as a rule. But she didn't trust herself to speak without stumbling over her own tongue.

"I think that's a good idea. Let me help you with that."

"No!" Gemma snapped. God, she didn't want him *helping*. She wanted to get away as fast as humanly possible. "Jason and I have got him."

Jason, who'd readily offered his assistance when she'd nearly face-planted off the stage with her brother, eyed Aaron with suspicion. "This guy hassling you?"

"No," said Gemma, suddenly exhausted. The last thing she needed was some kind of testosterone showdown. "He's fine. We're fine. Let's just get my brother outside." She glanced over.

Aaron was still there, still looking concerned, still looking delicious as ever with those broad shoulders her hands itched to stroke and that sensual mouth that had starred in countless sexy dreams.

"Let's go," said Gemma, tugging their little trio toward the exit.

Aaron skirted around them, moving to Jason and starting to reach for Rick. "Look, man, thanks for your help, but he's my friend. Why don't you let me—"

"We've *got this*," Gemma snarled, taking a firmer grip on her brother. "Thanks."

Aaron jolted back as if she'd slapped him, but Gemma was beyond caring. If she had her way, she'd never see him again, so it hardly mattered.

Almost a year. A year back in Memphis and she'd manage to avoid running into him. She could make that happen again. It wasn't like they ran in the same circles.

"Who's that?" mumbled Rick.

"No one important," she said softly. "C'mon. Just keep moving with us here."

Aaron fell back and let them pass. After the noisy, stuffy heat of the roadhouse, the cool air of the parking lot was a balm to Gemma's aching head.

"Rick, where did you park?"

He struggled to lift his head, squinting at the rows of vehicles. "Somewhere."

"What's he drive?" asked Jason.

"Black F150. Supercab."

That didn't narrow the field much. They both scanned the lot.

"That it? Back left corner. Two tone with the tan on the bottom?"

Gemma followed Jason's gaze. "Yeah. Come on, big brother. Let's get you home."

They skirted around the truck with steamed up windows, where the couple she'd seen on her arrival had disappeared. The light out here was lousy, not extending far beyond the pools cast by the floodlights mounted on the corner of the building. With a litany of silent prayers for her ankles and shoes, they made it to Rick's truck.

"I've got him," said Jason. "You get the door open."

Relinquishing Rick, Gemma unlocked the truck, pulled open the passenger side door. The seat was covered with files, his briefcase, and the other detritus he hadn't gotten around to stowing from the work days earlier in the week. Gemma shoved the lot of it into a banker's box in the floorboard and shifted the box into the backseat.

"There. Okay, Rick. In you go."

"He's out now."

Great. Gemma held in a string of curses. How the hell was she going to get him in the house? Maybe she'd just bring a blanket out to him and let him sleep it off in the truck.

She crawled into the backseat herself and pulled as Jason pushed. Between the two of them, they managed to get Rick and all his appendages into the truck and buckled in.

"Finally." Gemma took the hand Jason offered and climbed out of the narrow backseat. She turned to shut the suicide door. "Thanks for your help."

When she turned back around, Jason was inches away, mouth curved into a smile that raised the hair on Gemma's arms. "My pleasure," he said, planting his arms on either side of her to cage her against the truck. Alarms began to blare in her head as the first wash of fear had her heart beginning to pound.

"Um, look, Jason, I—"

"Just thought you might want to show your appreciation. I had a few ideas."

Obviously, she thought. Screw the shoes. The stiletto heels were practically weaponized. If one broke when she brought it down on his instep, so be it. But even as Gemma lifted her foot, Jason pulled back.

No, he was *being* pulled back.

Aaron spun Jason neatly away and placed himself in front of her as a shield. And damn it if that didn't just get her heart racing for a whole other reason.

"I expect you do have a few ideas," he said. "Let me go ahead and advise you that they're bad ones. A gentleman doesn't expect payment for helping a lady out. So why don't you go on back to Red's and find somebody more receptive to your advances."

For a moment, Gemma thought Jason was going to argue, but evidently he decided she wasn't worth it. With a rude remark under his breath, he turned and headed back for the bar.

Thank God.

Aaron watched him go, shoulders rigid until the other man went inside. Then he turned to her, eyes still hot. "You okay?"

"Yeah. Thanks for that."

She could see the temper warring on his face, waited for the confrontation about why she didn't want his help. Instead he said, "Rick's out cold. You'll never get him in the house on your own. I'm following you home."

Gemma opened her mouth but he interrupted before she could speak.

"Don't argue with me, Gemma. At least you know I won't try to molest you."

It made her feel small and petty. She hunched her shoulders defensively. "I wasn't going to argue. I was going to say thank you."

Aaron relaxed a bit. "Okay then. I'm parked on the drive. I'll follow you out."

Aaron's temper was at a steady boil by the time they made it back to Rick's place. He managed to keep a lid on it as they hauled Rick's dead weight out of the truck and into the house. Rick was already snoring by the time they poured him into bed.

Gemma tugged off his shoes. "Do you think it's safe to leave him? He's not so drunk he's going to have alcohol poisoning or something, right?"

"I saw him do that once in college, after Becky Winthrop dumped him. I don't think he's that far gone now," said Aaron.

"In that case, I hope he has the hangover from Hell tomorrow for putting me through this." With one last look of concern and irritation, she walked out of the bedroom.

Aaron held his tongue until they made it into the living room. "Now, how about you tell me what the hell is the matter with you?" he demanded.

Gemma stiffened and swung toward him from the cabinet Rick used as a bar, abandoning the bottle of wine she'd started to open. Her eyes had gone to slits. "Excuse me?"

"I've always thought you were one of the smartest women I've ever met. And tonight you were just being bone stupid. That asshole could've—" Aaron cut himself off, too easily able to see Jason caging her against the truck. "He could have hurt you. What would you have done if I hadn't been there?"

"I find a knee to the balls and a spiked heel to the instep to be pretty effective. Something you'll find out for yourself in short order if you don't back off right now."

Aaron realized he'd crowded into her space and stepped back immediately, hands lifted in truce. Unable to stay still, he started to pace. "I know you'd never have been in a place like that if Rick hadn't been a damned moron, and I'll take him to task for that when he's sober. But you." He looked at her standing there in her

New Year's Eve finery and shook his head. "What the hell were you thinking?"

"I was thinking I needed a hand getting Rick into the truck. Jason offered."

"So did I. And you know me, so exactly why was that redneck Neanderthal the preferable alternative?"

Gemma crossed her arms and paced to the window. "I didn't need your help. I'm not my brother's keeper and you aren't mine."

Where was this fury coming from? Baffled, Aaron scooped a hand through his hair. "What's wrong, Gemma?"

"You mean apart from the fact that my idiot brother decided to get so wasted I had to abandon my date at Chez Philippe midway through the entree in order to come rescue him, thus destroying any possibility that Victor will ever call me again?"

What the hell kind of name is Victor? Aaron wondered.

"This isn't about your date. I've never in my life known you to be foolish *or* rude. And you've been both tonight in the name of avoiding me."

"You don't know me, Aaron," Gemma spat. But she flinched and with it some of that icy reserve cracked. "I'm not avoiding you."

Aaron just looked at her, lifting a brow.

"Avoiding you makes it sound like we were in the same orbit to begin with. I haven't seen you in ten years, and there was absolutely no reason to think I ever would again."

"Rick's one of my best friends. Why wouldn't we have run into each other eventually?"

"Because I learned my lesson about hanging out with my brother's friends," she muttered.

"What's that supposed to mean?"

"Nothing. Look, I've had a craptastic night. I'm very sorry for being rude. There was no cause for that. I'm pissed off and you were the most readily available target. I thank you for your help with my brother. Now I'm sure you had your own New Year's plans that he interrupted, so you're welcome to go on back to them."

She didn't look at him during that little speech. It was so uncharacteristic of the girl he remembered, he felt compelled to push.

"Why do I get the feeling that there's something else going on here apart from the fact that Rick screwed up your date?"

Gemma took a bracing breath and let it out slow. "I didn't expect…this."

"Didn't expect what?"

She waved an impatient hand in his general direction. "You."

What the hell was that supposed to mean?

He took a step toward Gemma and watched her neatly sidestep him, reaching reflexively for the wine bottle and corkscrew to occupy her hands. She still wouldn't meet his eyes. His gaze skimmed down to the hollow of her throat, where he noted her pulse fluttering madly. The realization hit him like a Mack truck.

"You're nervous," he said in wonder. "I make

you nervous." Temper faded as he fought the smile that tugged as his lips.

She gave an irritated snort that he took as confirmation and neatly ripped off the foil covering the cork.

"You never used to be nervous around me."

A burst of self-deprecatory laughter escaped her. "Oh God, if you believe that, then I deserved an Oscar back then."

"What? Really?" He mentally replayed his memories of her, searching for signs of nerves.

She lifted the bottle, one hand on the embedded corkscrew, and held it like some kind of shield as she turned to face him, eyes fixed somewhere in the vicinity of his left shoulder. "You used to terrify me."

Used to? Aaron wondered. "I knew you had a little crush. It was sweet."

Gemma turned those winter gray eyes on him then and stared. "Sweet," she repeated, a world of insult vibrating in that one word.

Okay, there's a sensitive spot, he thought. "Is

that what this is about? What happened that summer?"

"I don't want to talk about it." She set down the wine, unopened, and turned to stare fixedly out the window.

"I think we *should* talk about it. Clear the air. I don't want things to be weird between us, Gemma."

"What does it matter if things are weird between us?"

"Because we used to be friends."

She snorted again.

"Well, sort of," he amended. "Look, there's no reason to let that amazing outfit of yours go to waste. Let's go out, see what we can salvage of the night. Let me buy you some dinner, a drink, and let's deal with...whatever this is. Please."

She pinched the bridge of her nose and huffed out a frustrated breath. "Fine. I might as well complete my mortification by *talking* about it and actually exorcising this demon."

"Look at it this way, if it doesn't work, you can go back to avoiding me."

Gemma cocked her head and flashed a glimmer of a smile. "There is that. Let me get my coat."

The place was a joint in the best sense of the word. Somewhere in Midtown, it was hidden and small, with no discernible name on the outside of the old, painted brick building. The interior was packed to the gills with patrons enjoying a wide variety of Memphis cuisine along with the live music pumping hot and moody from the tiny stage. The hostess led them to a high top table, where they ended up jammed elbow to elbow so that they could hear each other speak. That didn't do a damn thing for Gemma's nerves. She looked on the upcoming conversation like a root canal. Painful and necessary, and hopefully an experience never to be repeated. She was still cursing herself for being so *affected* by him. In all the day-dreams she'd had about seeing him again, not a single one included her being anything other than cool, calm, and collected, showing him in every possible way what he'd missed out on. None of them included him cluing in to her discomfort and cornering her into talking about it.

To put the discussion off, she peered at the menu and asked, "What's good here?"

"Everything. They're particularly famous for their ribs."

Gemma looked down at her white blouse. "I think no. What else?"

"Catfish. Burgers. And a seriously heart-stopping sausage po'boy."

As the least drippy option listed, she went with the catfish, blackened, and added a glass of Chardonnay. Aaron picked the po'boy and a beer.

She waited until the waitress returned with their drinks to speak again. Because of the music, she had to lean into his space, close enough to see the dark flecks in his blue eyes. "The music is great!"

"This group is a particular favorite of mine. Old school covers. They favor Howlin' Wolf, John Lee Hooker, and, of course, B.B. And they mix it up a bit with original stuff too. You a blues fan?"

"I don't know it well, but I like it." Gemma took a breath and braced herself. "Look, I want to apologize again for being bitchy earlier. You were trying to help, and it was rude of me to take out my frustration on you."

"Is that your way of trying to welch on our discussion?"

"No. It just bears saying. I can admit when I've behaved badly."

Aaron smiled at that and her pulse gave a hard stutter. "There's the direct and forthright girl I remember."

She grimaced. "That's gotten me into more trouble over the years."

"I appreciate a woman who says what she means. Takes the complication and guesswork out of things. You never played games."

"I suck at it. And I'm not going to start now. I promised we could talk about that summer and clear the air." *Because I've lost my mind.*

"Maybe I should start," he said.

"No. No, this is on me. I need to get it out before I lose my nerve." She took a bracing swallow of wine, winced a little at the burn. "I guess for this to make sense, I have to give you some context. You didn't know me outside of what you saw at the lake."

"You didn't strike me as the kind of girl who tried on personalities like outfits."

"No, I wasn't. I'm not. But people are different in different settings. I was easier at the lake. More comfortable and free to be myself. Back home, in school, well, that was a whole other story. High school was hell for me. I mean, sure, it was fine academically. I excelled at that. You already know I come from a bright family, and I didn't fall far from the tree. But everything that made me a success as a student made me a freak to most of my peers."

"You were not a freak."

His ready defense made her smile a little. "High school boys thought I was. I was smart and didn't see the need to hide it. I wasn't properly demure and self-effacing like other girls. So they were afraid of me."

"The ego of a teenage boy is a fragile thing. I can see how you might've intimidated them a bit."

Gemma shrugged, sipped at her wine. "Teenage girls aren't any better. Anyway, on the heels of the latest rejection on that front, I went to the lake that summer, and Rick brought you. You were different."

She stroked a thumb along the stem of her wineglass and thought back to the first time she'd seen Aaron. It'd been like looking on Apollo with that smile. He'd dazzled her. He could still dazzle her.

"I was older."

"Yeah." Gemma nodded in acknowledgment. "Yeah, you were. I guess that was the point at which I really understood exactly how true that whole thing is about girls maturing faster than boys. Being around you was so refreshing. You didn't look at me like I had a second head when I expressed an opinion. You listened and respected what I said. A lot of other guys would've automatically relegated me into annoying kid sister status, but you didn't."

"You didn't act like a kid, and I'm pretty sure that big brain of yours had a good ten years on the rest of us. That was only annoying the fifth or sixth time you whipped my ass at Trivial Pursuit."

She chuckled. "You were easy prey. Everybody else in the family knew never to play me at trivia games."

"I enjoyed your company."

"I know. It showed. I guess under the circumstances, it was inevitable that I'd fall for you." Gemma couldn't look at him, couldn't bear to see any expression of pity or discomfort. But she'd push through the rest of it. "I was turning sixteen in August and I didn't want to be a cliche, so I decided to do something about it."

"Midnight Twister," he murmured.

So he did remember. Eyes on her wine, she continued, "I knew Rick would bail on it. He sucks at Twister and gets mad because all my gymnastics training meant I was more flexible than him. It was an effective tactic for getting you into close quarters. It took every shred of courage I had to try to kiss you, and as soon as you clued in, you couldn't get away fast enough. It was absolutely humiliating. Though this particular moment is climbing the rankings on that score," she admitted. She took another gulp of wine and wished it would work faster. "I felt like a complete *idiot.* So much so, that I left so I wouldn't have to face you again." And boy it had taken some fast talking to her mom to manage that in under twenty-four hours.

"Gemma." Sympathy in his tone. Pity, probably. God, she didn't want his pity. Not then and, certainly, not now

She shrugged, determined to play it down.

"It wasn't a big deal in the long run. I grew up, went to college where my brain was actually considered an asset. But seeing you again makes me *feel*...fifteen and stupid again. So you'll have to forgive me for being awkward and kind of rude about this."

"I'm sorry." What else could he say but that? In his own rush for self-preservation, he'd hurt her.

Color rode high in Gemma's cheeks and she refused to look at him. He had to fix this.

"I wish you'd stayed." Aaron laid a hand over hers, felt her fingers jump.

Her eyes cut to their linked hands before looking away again. "Why?"

"So I could've at least explained."

"You didn't owe me an explanation. It was obvious enough."

He'd thought it was, but if she'd spent all these years blaming herself, maybe she hadn't actually noticed. "It wasn't you. At least not for the reasons you think." If she bared her embarrassment, he could bare his.

"What? Did you have a girlfriend you'd neglected to mention?" she scoffed.

"No. Do you have any idea how hard I had to work to remember who you were?"

Now she did look at him, brow furrowed. "Who I was?"

"Your family invited me out to your cabin. You were Rick's little sister. I was not supposed to notice you beyond that. But you were smart and funny and had these legs that should've been illegal."

He'd wanted that direct gaze again, and he had it. "You noticed my legs?"

"Hard not to. I've got eyes in my head, don't I?"

"They're just legs. You stand on them."

"Trust me when I tell you, they're not just legs. Which is neither here nor there, because I shouldn't have noticed them, shouldn't have thought about them or you."

"Why?"

"Because no matter how mature you were, you were *fifteen.* I was twenty. Way too old for you. If Rick had known what went through my head when I looked at you, he'd have been duty-bound to kick my ass. And he'd have been absolutely right to do it."

Gemma stared at him, as if she couldn't quite process what he'd said. "You...actually *liked* me?"

Like. Such a pale, innocent sort of word. It felt less damning than the alternatives.

"Yes, I liked you."

"Then why..."

"That game of Twister got us in close quarters, exactly as you intended." He'd ended up pinned beneath her. "You started to kiss me and I had a...very...human response."

"Running away was a human response?"

"Gemma," he said, exasperated, "you're a smart woman. I find you incredibly attractive. My very human response to that was why I essentially ran away." And if she didn't stop looking at him like that, he was going to have another. Shifting in his chair, Aaron took a swig of his beer to wet his dry mouth.

He saw the moment she caught on. Her eyes widened and her mouth dropped open. "Oh." A faint flush of color bloomed across her cheeks.

"It was completely and totally inappropriate, and *I* was embarrassed. So I jumped ship. It was never about you doing anything wrong."

"Well," she said after a pause, "that's…illuminating."

God. He actually felt the embarrassment crawling up his neck and twitched his shoulders as if he could shrug it off. "When I found out you were gone, I thought you left because you were…freaked out or thought I was trying something. I didn't want you to think I was taking advantage."

The look she shot him was full of more insult. "I was fifteen, not a child. Perfectly capable of saying no. Or yes, for that matter."

"I couldn't afford to even *think* about you saying yes. You were jailbait. Smart, funny, attractive jailbait. You can let that insult you all you want, but it doesn't change the facts."

Gemma studied him over the rim of her glass. "Probably good you didn't say that back then. Everybody treated me as an adult from so early on, that would've just pissed me off to no end. I wanted to be taken seriously."

"Acting adult and being adult are two different things. And believe me, I took that damned seriously."

After a long silence, she nodded, "Fair enough."

Aaron considered them even on the mortification scale for the night. He lifted his beer. "To our mutual embarrassment. May we now be able to get past it."

"I'll drink to that." Gemma touched her glass to his.

The charged moment was broken by the arrival of their meal. In the wake of their server's departure, a new layer of awkward seemed to descend. Aaron floundered for a good way to break it. "So," he began, "tell me about this Victor guy."

Smooth, Hendricks. Because you really want to hear about the other dude she's into.

"He's an art dealer," said Gemma.

Aaron's brows winged up. "An art dealer. Not what I expected. Are you into that kind of thing? Shows and galleries and whatnot?"

"Not generally. But a good friend of mine is a metal sculptor. She recently had a show at a little gallery downtown. I went to be supportive and met Victor. He was…amused by my interpretations of the structures as an engineer. He was charming and attentive, so when he asked me out for tonight, I said yes."

"Exactly how broken up are you that Rick blew your shot with him?"

Her lips quirked. "Subtle." She shifted in her chair to cross those amazing legs and Aaron had some difficulty keeping his eyes off them. "I'm far too literal and grounded for the art crowd. Rick probably did me a favor. And if you tell him so, I'll call you a dirty, dog liar. He's still absolutely on my shit list for being an idiot. But I can't see myself being with anyone long term who would expect me to put a swanky dinner over the welfare of family. Victor wasn't concerned. He didn't even offer to come with me."

"Jerk."

She tipped her head in acknowledgment. "Enough about me and my lousy date. What about you? Why aren't you out on the town with some hottie tonight?"

Aaron smiled. "Last time I checked, I was."

God, she was so cute when her cheeks pinked like that.

"You know what I mean," she said. "Why weren't you out on a date yourself when you got the call? Or were you?"

"I was playing through *Call of Duty* for the twenty-seventh time, so no great loss." He shrugged. "I don't know. New Year's Eve dates seem to carry so much more weight than normal dates. There's all that expectation of a midnight kiss, and all this meaning attached to it. Like those are the lips you're supposed to be kissing the rest of the next year. And if the date bombs, then there you are with a lousy start to the new year. It seemed safer all around to just stay in."

"In that case, I'm glad things tanked with Victor. That's a lot of pressure on one kiss."

"Exactly. There wasn't anybody I felt like jumping off that bridge with, so I opted to stay in." And thank God he'd been there to get the message.

The sting of embarrassment had faded by the time they made it through their meal. Maybe because they'd finally cleared the air. Or maybe because the waitress brought a second glass of wine to replace the one she'd drained.

"Better?" Aaron asked.

Knowing he saw too much, she shrugged and admitted, "You still make me nervous."

"Well, there's one, sure-fire way to fix that." He plucked the glass from her hand.

"What's that?"

"Immersion therapy," he said, shoving back from the table. "Come dance with me."

She hesitated only a moment before taking his hand and following him out onto the tiny, packed dance floor. As guitars wailed and the singer crooned, he slid his arms around her. The pulse hammered in her throat as he nudged her into the rhythm of the music. Gemma was stiff and clumsy, her body seeming to jolt with his every touch.

"Loosen up, Gem. This is supposed to be fun."

Fun. Right. She breathed out a long sigh and focused on progressively relaxing her muscles. It was a tough job with her inner teenager going *OMG, you're dancing with Aaron Hendricks!* But after a couple of songs, she loosened up enough that he got more ambitious than a simple circle and sway. With a burst of momentum, Aaron spun Gemma out, then twirled her back more firmly against his body. In the heels she was almost eye level with him.

"How're those nerves doing?" he asked.

They were sparking like fireworks, but she'd recovered enough to pull the mantle of calm and maturity back around her. "Better."

"Good. That makes one of us."

"One of us?" She arched a brow in question.

"See, I've made an important observation over the last couple of hours."

"What's that?"

"You're not fifteen anymore," Aaron dropped his gaze to her lips, "and I find the woman every bit as appealing as the girl."

"Do you, now?" Gemma's tone was playful, though the rumba in her stomach had transitioned into an Irish river dance.

Somehow, when she'd stepped into Red's, she had crossed into a parallel universe. There was no other explanation for how her greatest teenage fantasy had sprung to life out of the ashes of one of the worst nights of her adult life. How could she possibly have imagined that their awkward conversation would lead to *this?* She never dreamed that her attraction to him could be mutual. *Had* been mutual, even back then.

"If you're not on the same page here, this'd probably be a good time to mention it," said Aaron, not letting her go as the song ended.

Not on the same page? Was he kidding?

"Do you see me running?" she asked.

From the stage, the singer encouraged everybody to grab their honey. Dimly, Gemma was aware of him beginning the countdown.

"Ten...Nine..."

If I'm dreaming, I don't wanna wake up, she thought, her pulse starting to thrum slow and thick as his blue eyes went dark.

"Five...Four..."

Aaron tugged her closer. The breath seemed to clog in her chest as the crowd around them picked up the chant.

"Three...Two...One...Happy New Year!"

Anticipation gave way to a stunned delight as he settled his mouth over hers. Heat rolled through her, bubbling up in a purr of pleasure against his lips. Gemma had never in her life been more grateful for the slow, easy pace of the South. Aaron kissed her with the focused patience of a man who knew how to savor, and she gloried in it, changing the angle to deepen the kiss. Her arms slid around his shoulders, banding there even as his arms tightened around her. How could he incite such a storm inside her with only his mouth?

As the singer's smoky voice launched into a new number and lulled them into a lazy sway, Aaron eased back again, allowing scant inches between them.

"Well, that was certainly worth the wait," she managed.

"If you were any other woman, I'd be mentioning how my place is twenty minutes from here."

With her blood still roaring, Gemma wished she was any other woman. But whatever flared between them wouldn't be simple and the potential fallout would affect more than just the two of them. "More's the pity," she said, giving in to the shiver as he stroked a hand down her back. "I really like your mouth."

Aaron gave a strangled laugh and dropped his temple to hers. "Don't say stuff like that. It makes me want to use it on every inch of you."

"Oh, God." Gemma closed her eyes and rode out the blast of lust that shot through her. "Don't say stuff like that. It makes me want to let you."

"How do you want to proceed with this?" he asked.

Straight to your bed. Do not pass Go, do not collect $200. She swallowed. "Carefully, I think. Very carefully."

"Okay then." Aaron tugged her closer and rested his cheek against hers.

She could feel his heart pounding against hers, but he kept his hold easy, as if this were nothing more complicated than a dance. When the song was over, he led her back to their table and kept her hand in his as they sat.

"You want dessert?" he asked.

"Maybe later."

"You want me to take you home?"

And put an end to the dream? Gemma shook her head, and Aaron's lips curved in that slow smile that made her heart skip a beat.

"Then give me tonight. Let me show you Memphis as it's meant to be experienced."

How could she say no to that?

Aaron took Gemma dancing on Beale Street. They moved from club to club, sampling the best music Memphis had to offer. The energy of the New Year's Eve crowds banished the sense of nagging exhaustion that might have brought the night to an end. When they ran out of steam, he took her to Gibson's for fresh donuts. They talked for hours over an endless pot of coffee, catching up on years and playing footsie beneath the table. Dawn found them walking in a park beside the river, arm-in-arm and easy with each other.

As the sky began to lighten behind the city skyline, Aaron tugged Gemma over to a bench to sit and watch. The wind off the water behind them was frigid, and she burrowed into him, resting her head against his shoulder. He pressed a kiss to the top of her head.

"Tired?"

"Mmm. I'm so tired, I'm wired. I think if we stop moving for very long, I'm going to crash and burn. I can't remember the last time I stayed up all night."

"Grad school, for me," said Aaron. "And certainly it wasn't for anything as pleasant as this."

"It's like that movie," she said.

"What movie?"

"*Before Sunrise.* The movie that made every teenage girl fall in love with Ethan Hawke back in the 90s. He and Julie Delpy's character meet on the train and end up spending all night wandering some city in Austria. Vienna, I think. Can't remember. Anyway, they get this one, amazing night together before she has to get on the train to go back to Paris and he has to get to the airport to fly home."

"Is that all I'm going to get with you, Gemma? One night?"

She lifted her head to face him. "This has been one of the best nights of my life. You've made one of my greatest teenage fantasies come to life, and I don't know how to thank you for that."

It sounded too much like the preface of an apology. "I sense a 'but' coming on."

"But we have to face reality."

Aaron braced himself, already feeling the lash of disappointment. "And what's the reality?"

"The reality is…this is complicated." Gemma gave a rueful smile and cupped his cheek. "I'm crazy about you. I've always been crazy about you. But you're Rick's best friend."

"Do you think he would have a problem with this?" He stroked a thumb over her knuckles.

Gemma considered the question. "I think it

would surprise the hell out of him. But a problem? I don't know. He was never one of those hugely overprotective big brothers. There was such an age gap between us, there wasn't really opportunity or need. And certainly, at this point, you and I are both unattached adults."

"A fact for which I find myself incredibly grateful, at the moment."

"Do you really care what my brother thinks?"

"Do you?" Aaron countered.

"Technically, whatever we do is none of his damned business," she pointed out. "But I wouldn't want to be the cause of any rift between you. You've been friends a long time."

"I don't think Rick would be small enough to try and pull the protective big brother routine now, not if we were really serious about this," said Aaron. He continued to play with her fingers as he fixed his gaze on hers. "So I guess the question is, how serious are we?"

"How can we even answer that?" asked Gemma. "All we know at this point is that we have chemistry. Really *great* chemistry," she qualified.

"That's not all we know," he argued. "We know we enjoy each other's company. That you're not a half bad dancer when you can give up control and let somebody else lead."

She laughed.

"We know we like the same kind of donuts and that you taste delicious with powdered sugar." He nipped in to kiss the corner of her mouth, as if he'd missed a spot the last time. "We know that, once we get going, we can talk all night without running out of things to say. We also know that neither of us would be content with one night of no-strings-attached sex."

Gemma blinked, her brows arching in surprise. "And you say I'm direct."

"Calling it like I see it," he said easily. "Whatever this is between us, it's more than just an itch to be scratched and forgotten. Do you disagree?"

"No," she shook her head. "No, I don't. No

matter how earth-shattering I suspect that night would be."

Aaron grinned. "Careful. You'll give me ideas."

"Somehow, I don't think you need any help in that department," she said.

"I kissed you at midnight," he pointed out.

"You did," she acknowledged. "And I keep worrying that any minute now, I'm going to wake up and find out that this is all some kind of crazy, whacked out dream."

"Then stay asleep with me," said Aaron. "Today, tomorrow. The rest of the year." *The rest of my life.* "However long we might last, I'd rather be dreaming with you than be awake with anyone else."

Gemma pressed her free hand to her heart and sighed. "Who knew you were such a romantic?"

"You did. I believe you lobbed that charge at me while we looked at stars over the lake that summer."

"You vehemently denied the accusation, as I recall."

"Of course, I did. My man cred with Rick was at stake. And I didn't want him thinking I had ideas about you."

"You have ideas now," she said.

"I certainly do. So how 'bout it?"

"It just so happens I like the way you think." Gemma leaned forward and brushed her lips lightly over his. "Take me home, Hendricks. If you play your cards right, I just might cook you some breakfast."

Finis.

Copyright 2014 by Kait Nolan

OTHER BOOKS BY KAIT NOLAN

A complete and up-to-date list of all my books can be found at https://kaitnolan.com.

THE MISFIT INN SERIES
SMALL TOWN FAMILY ROMANCE

- *When You Got A Good Thing* (Kennedy and Xander)
- *Til There Was You* (Misty and Denver)

- *Those Sweet Words* (Pru and Flynn)
- *Stay A Little Longer* (Athena and Logan)
- *Bring It On Home* (Maggie and Porter)

RESCUE MY HEART SERIES
SMALL TOWN MILITARY ROMANCE

- *Baby It's Cold Outside* (Ivy and Harrison)
- *What I Like About You* (Laurel and Sebastian)
- *Bad Case of Loving You* (Paisley and Ty prequel)
- *Made For Loving You* (Paisley and Ty)

MEN OF THE MISFIT INN
SMALL TOWN SOUTHERN ROMANCE

- *Let It Be Me* (Emerson and Caleb)
- *Our Kind of Love* (Abbey and Kyle)

WISHFUL SERIES

SMALL TOWN SOUTHERN ROMANCE

- *Once Upon A Coffee* (Avery and Dillon)
- *To Get Me To You* (Cam and Norah)
- *Know Me Well* (Liam and Riley)
- *Be Careful, It's My Heart* (Brody and Tyler)
- *Just For This Moment* (Myles and Piper)
- *Wish I Might* (Reed and Cecily)
- *Turn My World Around* (Tucker and Corinne)
- *Dance Me A Dream* (Jace and Tara)
- *See You Again* (Trey and Sandy)
- *The Christmas Fountain* (Chad and Mary Alice)
- *You Were Meant For Me* (Mitch and Tess)
- *A Lot Like Christmas* (Ryan and Hannah)
- *Dancing Away With My Heart* (Zach and Lexi)

WISHING FOR A HERO SERIES (A WISHFUL SPINOFF SERIES)
SMALL TOWN ROMANTIC SUSPENSE

- *Make You Feel My Love* (Judd and Autumn)
- *Watch Over Me* (Nash and Rowan)
- *Can't Take My Eyes Off You* (Ethan and Miranda)
- *Burn For You* (Sean and Delaney)

MEET CUTE ROMANCE
SMALL TOWN SHORT ROMANCE

- *Once Upon A Snow Day*
- *Once Upon A New Year's Eve*
- *Once Upon An Heirloom*
- *Once Upon A Coffee*
- *Once Upon A Campfire*
- *Once Upon A Rescue*

SUMMER CAMP
CONTEMPORARY ROMANCE

- *Once Upon A Campfire*
- *Second Chance Summer*

ABOUT KAIT

Kait is a Mississippi native, who often swears like a sailor, calls everyone sugar, honey, or darlin', and can wield a bless your heart like a saber or a Snuggie, depending on requirements.

You can find more information on this

RITA ® Award-winning author and her books on her website http://kaitnolan.com. While you're there, sign up for her newsletter so you don't miss out on news about new releases!

www.ingramcontent.com/pod-product-compliance
Lightning Source LLC
Chambersburg PA
CBHW070525100726
47907CB00004B/982